HEART OF DISASTER

RACHEL WESSON

DEDICATION

If you ever visit Ireland, you will find numerous reminders of those who traveled on the Titanic. The exhibition in Belfast and the museum in Cobh, Co. Cork (Queenstown in the book as that was its name under the English), are the two biggest ones. There are memorials in Galway, Mayo, and other areas where large groups of Irish people left, never to return. There were many heroes on board that night, some whose names we know and some, whose stories never saw the light of day.

According to my grandmother, Annie O'Callaghan (nee McGann), we had a family member who survived the sinking of the Titanic. Unfortunately, I wasn't interested in family history back then. And now her generation has passed, nobody can remember the person's name.

To those whose selfless acts saved dozens of people on the Titanic. To those who survived and all those who died on the RMS Titanic. May you rest in peace.

CHAPTER 1

TUESDAY, APRIL 9TH, 1912, BALLINASLOE, CO GALWAY

*W*ith tears streaming down her face, Kate milked the cow in the barn. The animal seemed to sense her distress, as she kept trying to butt Kate with her head. Kate had fallen back into the hay a couple of times, spilling the milk from the pail.

"Kate Maloney, enough of that. You will turn the milk sour, what's left of it."

Kate almost fell off the milking stool at the sound of her adoptive grandmother's irritated voice. It was so unlike Nell. The old woman put aside the broom she had been using and pushed Kate out of the way. Nell's twisted, old hands soothed the animal, and the milk ran freely into the pail.

"Nell, I don't want to go to America. I want to stay here with you on this farm."

"You have to go, Kate. This farm isn't big enough to support both of us. You're young. You deserve more than trying to eek a living out of this ground. Your parents,

God rest them, would want more for you." Nell finished the milking, and wiped her hands before taking Kate's hand, her voice softer now, "I know you are scared my darling girl, but you will be fine. America is full of opportunities and someday you will be able to come back and buy up land around here for miles around. You'll wear the latest fashions and stylish hats. You'll have all the old ones here staring at you. Now come on, dry your eyes. We have work to be done before we go to your party."

"The wake, you mean."

"The American wake, nobody's died girl, and, for that, we must be thankful."

Kate didn't share Nell's views. She hated normal wakes, thinking it creepy to have a dead body in the house while everyone prayed, drank, and made music around the deceased. The family and friends mourned together with the villagers, who also wanted to mark the person's passing or just fancied a drink at someone else's expense. She knew people going to America rarely returned, hence the term American Wake. The people wanted to mourn those leaving, but it still was rather weird to take part in your own wake.

CHAPTER 2

*L*ater that evening, Kate, watched as her relatives and friends danced the night away outside the Madden's house. Michael and Fiona Madden were Nell's closest neighbors.

"Evening, Kate."

"Evening, Mrs. Madden." Just as Kate returned the greeting, Cathy and Seamus danced past them.

"Mam, you should be dancing," Cathy called.

"Go away with ya, girl. I'm too old." Mrs. Madden tore her gaze from her daughter. "I still can't believe my two youngest are on their way to America. It's a sad day for Ballinasloe, so it is."

Kate swallowed hard, trying not to feel guilty. She was thrilled Cathy Madden was coming with her to America. She didn't think she would be brave enough to leave her behind.

"Kate, look at that eejit, Daniel Donnelly. He will

have his poor mother in an early grave. Martha is too old for dancing that fast."

Kate glanced at the dancers. Mrs. Donnelly, was red-cheeked, as she gripped Daniel's arm.

"I think he is trying to distract his mam," Kate said.

Mrs. Madden smiled. She put her arm around Kate and squeezed her close. "You've got a kind heart, Kate. Don't ever change." Mrs. Madden coughed and moved away. "I best get inside and see how much whiskey my fella has had. He will miss Cathy something dreadful."

Mrs. Madden had reason to be concerned. The drink was flowing almost as fast as the women's tears. Kate saw a number of men with suspiciously bright eyes, but none of them would be seen crying in public. Nell ambled over to her.

"Why are you not dancing, Kate?" Nell asked, fingering a piece of paper. Kate recognized the advertisement. Daniel had shown her earlier; it outlined the attractions of the steerage accommodation on RMS Titanic. Kate panicked. She didn't think she could discuss anything about the ship. She caught Daniel's eye. He strode over and held out his hand.

"Kate, would you like to dance?"

Only then did Daniel appear to notice Nell. He flushed. "Sorry Nell, I didn't mean to intrude on your time with Kate."

"Don't mind me, son. I've been reading the paper you gave to your mam."

Kate hid a smile. Most everyone knew Nell couldn't

read. It wasn't unusual given her age. But the old lady had her pride.

"Did you see the food menu? It made me mouth water, so it did. I don't think I will get off the ship in America. With food like that, I could stay on the Titanic forever."

"Daniel Donnelly! Typical man thinking with your stomach." Nell's eyes sparkled, as she admonished him. "Your brother, Sean, will be thrilled to see ye. Tell him, he owes me a letter. He must have found a younger woman to replace me."

Kate and Daniel exchanged a smile at Nell's joke. The old woman was about fifty years older than Sean Donnelly. Kate had vague memories attending the American Wake for the elder Donnelly boys.

"Who could replace you, Nell?" Daniel glanced at Kate. "I can't think of how many American wakes I've attended, and now it's our turn."

Silence lingered. Kate blinked rapidly to stop her tears. She couldn't look at Nell.

Nell cleared her throat. "Tell me more about the *RMS Titanic*. From what your mam says, it sounds like a posh hotel." Nell cackled before sniffing some snuff. "Not that I would know anything about hotels. Never stepped foot in one."

"I'm not one for hotels either, so can't really compare. Most ships don't offer a dining room in steerage. The Titanic has one with wooden tables and benches. Myself and Seamus are sharing a four-berth cabin. The men have a smoking room, and the women have a room for reading or whatnot. We don't have to bring our own food."

"'Tis back to your stomach. Kate, take the hint. Go find young Daniel something to eat. He can keep me company."

Grateful for a chance to compose herself, Kate went in search of some sandwiches. When she returned, Nell was sitting alone. Nell looked up, as Kate walked toward her.

"His mam called him. I guess she wanted some time alone with her son."

Kate struggled to find her voice, because of the lump in her throat. Her hand shook, as she handed Nell the plate of sandwiches. Nell's fingers grazed hers. Kate looked up to find the old lady staring at her. It was now or never.

"I can't believe, I'm going. I know, I should count my lucky stars and be grateful for my good fortune, but I don't want to leave. I want to live here with you."

"Aw now, Kate," Nell's work-worn hands grasped Kate's arm. "You got to go, love. You have a chance at a great life. Sure, haven't all the ones coming home from America talked about the great time they have over there? The chances to make something of themselves. What have you got to look forward to here?"

Unbidden, her eyes glanced toward Francis Blake, the man Kate had worshipped since she was knee-high to a grasshopper. She shuddered at how close she had come to making a mistake.

Nell misread Kate's reaction as a longing for Francis.

"Now, love, you can't have him and that's that. The son of an English landowner is never going to settle down with a local girl. No point in crying over spilled milk." Nell looked in Blake's direction and spat some snuff on the floor. "He was never the man for you. Your poor father would be spinning in his grave, if he even knew you were looking in that direction. After what those English did to us? Sure, isn't it their fault you find yourself on the way to America? If they had left your poor daddy alone, you and your mam could have lived here forever."

Kate had never told Nell about what Francis Blake had tried to do. She'd been too afraid of what Nell might do. The woman was old, but she had connections with those fighting for Ireland's freedom. Nell would have been horrified, if she knew what had almost happened, and her reactions could have landed the old woman in trouble with the law. It was best for everyone that Kate and Cathy had kept the details of that horrible day to themselves.

Kate still believed you shouldn't judge someone by where they came from, so she tried to shut out Nell's voice. Nell went on her favorite rant about the English landlords and how they had destroyed Ireland. She counted to ten, as Nell started on her favorite subject, the famine.

"I remember when I was a young one and the roads were covered in people dying from hunger. What did those English swine do to help the starving? Did they give us food? Like heck they did. They put the brave

7

men who tried to do the right thing for their families in prison or worse. Shipped them off to godforsaken lands in Australia. And for what? Fishing in a stream on their land or catching a rabbit for the pot. What did they expect the men to do with hungry children begging for food? Those Blakes did nothing. With their fancy clothes and big houses. Mark my words, my girl, it's better off you are in America. There, everyone is equal. It doesn't matter whether you are Irish or not. They treat everyone the same."

Desperate to escape the old lady's lecture but not wanting to cause her pain, she looked around the room and sighed with relief, when she spotted her best friend and fellow-traveler.

"Nell, there's Cathy. I just want to ask her something about the voyage. I will be back in a few minutes."

Kate ran rather than walked over to her friend.

"Are you all right, Kate? You look a bit flushed," Cathy said. She knew how Kate felt about Francis Blake and probably assumed she was flustered due to his presence. "Daddy had to invite Blake, although I don't think anyone believed he would come."

"It's not Blake. I don't care about that idiot. He knows to stay away from me. It's this." Kate waved her hands around.

"What do you mean?"

"Cathy, I got to get out of here. It's giving me the chills. It's like someone died."

Cathy burst out laughing, something that didn't sit well with Kate. She pouted as Cathy kept on laughing.

"It is a wake. Sure, when will we ever see this lot again?" Cathy remarked before saying sternly, "Kate, take that look off your face, and act your age. These people need to mark our going. Can't you see it's killing them to say goodbye to their loved ones knowing they probably will never see them again? Look at Mrs. Donnelly. The poor woman has lost eleven children in all, three dead, two in jail in England and six in America. Now her favorite, Daniel, is off to America. The woman's heart is broken."

CHAPTER 3

*K*ate closed her eyes, taking a deep painful breath, as guilt overwhelmed her. What Cathy said was true. The men and women of their village were showing them respect by giving them a living wake.

"I'm an ungrateful brat, aren't I?" Kate sat on the grass, her face in her hands.

"You're not. You're upset."

"I am. All these people used the few pennies they had and some they didn't to put together this feast. I've moaned to Nell when the old woman has been like a mother and grandmother combined."

"Nell loves you."

"I know. Look at how I repaid her. She probably regrets taking me in."

"Kate Maloney, that's enough. Nell loves the bones of you. You are the granddaughter she never had. It isn't just because the British soldiers killed your daddy at the same time as Nell's sons. Guilt hasn't made her feed and shelter you. She loves you."

Kate couldn't speak.

"Nell kept you at school when the rest of us were all out working to help our families. The best thing you can do is get a great job and send her home some money, not sit around sulking."

Kate clenched her fists, her nails biting into her palms.

"Kate, I'm not trying to upset you. You said Nell was terrified of going into the workhouse when she gets older. You can help her, if you go to America. Get a good job and earn lots of money. When Nell is too old to live alone, you can pay someone to give her a roof over her head."

Kate brushed the tears from her eyes. Cathy was right. Nell had spoken of her dread of ending up in the workhouse. Kate could make sure Nell had shelter. She stood and pulled Cathy to her feet. She hugged Cathy, surprising her friend.

"What was that in aid of?" Cathy said crossly, obviously embarrassed by the public show of affection.

"I am so happy you're coming with me. I could never say goodbye to you," Kate replied. "You're right as usual. I'm being selfish and not thinking of Nell and the rest of the people I love. Forgive me."

She didn't wait for Cathy's answer but went back to where Nell was sitting and threw her arms around the old lady.

"I'm sorry for being such a wet blanket earlier. I am going to miss you, Granny Nell."

She felt Nell shudder with emotion. She hugged her closer, knowing it was unlikely they would see each other again.

"I will miss you too, *Alannah*."

Nell's use of the Gaelic term for loved one almost broke Kate's resolve. Kate straightened her shoulders. She had to be brave. Nell continued speaking.

"You will have to write me lots of letters. Father Curry will read them to me. Promise me you will."

"I promise, Nell. I will send you the best shawl ever to keep you warm in the winter months."

"That would be nice, Kate love." Nell dabbed her eyes with the corner of a rather dirty looking hanky. "Now go on and dance. Let me see you smiling and having the craic. That's how I want to remember you, girl, having fun."

Kate didn't need to be told twice. She danced with just about every man in the village, including Father Curry who waltzed her around the room. He stank of whiskey.

"Look after Nell for me, won't you, Father?"

"I will indeed, Kate. Sure, the woman will still be alive when I am six feet under."

"I don't know about that, Father. Nell likes to pretend she is younger than she is. She never complains, but I've seen how much effort it takes for her to get out of bed. Her hands shake with age."

"Don't fret, Kate. I'll call on Nell often, as will Martha. Martha will need something to distract her."

"Thank you, Father."

"Kate, you will remember your faith, won't you?" Father Curry looked serious for a moment, pushing a mop of graying hair back from his sweat-covered face. "America is a good place, but there are plenty of distractions for a young girl like yourself."

"I will, Father."

"I know you think I am just an old priest, but I know the ways of the world and the temptations available. So, stay away from the drink, and keep your virtue."

Kate didn't comment on the irony of being told to avoid alcohol by someone who smelled like he slept in a vat of it.

CHAPTER 4

The next morning, Kate woke early, but Nell was still up before her, standing at the fire stirring the porridge. Kate washed and dressed before sitting at the small table to eat her breakfast. She swallowed hard to get rid of the lump in her throat.

Nell tapped Kate on the shoulder. "Eat up, now, you have a long journey ahead of you. It was mighty good of Cathy's father to offer to drive you to Galway. He had his head screwed on the right way when he asked the Burkes to allow you to share their lift. Traveling as a group and sharing costs will keep expenses down. You will need every bit of your savings when you get to America."

Kate couldn't speak. She swallowed the oatmeal, not tasting any of it. She wasn't hungry, but she couldn't offend Nell by refusing to eat.

Nell stirred the pot on the fire.

"I couldn't believe it, when I heard Margaret and the children were going to America with John Burke. It will be a huge change for all of them. Ruth and Niamh will probably be upset at leaving their friends, but sure they are bound to meet new ones."

Kate ate as Nell filled the silence with chatter.

"Want more?" Nell asked, when finally Kate finished the last of her oatmeal.

"No, thank you, Nell." Kate stood up. She hated goodbyes at the best of times, but she couldn't wrap her head around the fact that this was it. She would never see this woman again. Nell took something from the box she kept on the shelf above her bed.

"I got something for you. Don't be telling Father Curry, as he doesn't approve of superstitious nonsense, as he calls it. But keep this about you, all the time. You hear?"

Nell handed her a small bag and her rosary beads.

"Yes, Nell." Kate took the small bag, but she wasn't about to take Nell's favorite rosary beads. "I can't take these," she protested.

"You can, and you will. Your mother, God rest her soul, gave them to me when you were born. She'd want you to have them."

Kate couldn't respond. She put the rosary beads into her pocket before opening the small bag. She looked up in surprise when she saw the clay inside. "You want me to bring some dirt with me?"

"Dirt! It's not dirt from the yard, you silly girl. It's clay from St Mogue's shrine to keep you safe from drowning or boilers. My father, God rest his soul, used to take it with him out on the boat, and he died in his own bed."

"But, Nell, they said the *Titanic* is a giant ship; it will be safe won't it?" Kate's stomach had a whole heap of butterflies dancing around in it.

"Sure, it will." The old woman couldn't mask the concern in her eyes. "But it doesn't hurt anyone to be careful. Take it with you. It's all I got to give you. That and the love I hold for you in here." Nell pointed at her chest, her eyes suspiciously bright.

Kate couldn't remember ever seeing Nell cry. Locals said she hadn't shed a tear at her own children's funeral. Both Nell's sons had died with Kate's father in a skirmish against the British.

Kate hugged her. "I promise to keep them both close to me. I love you."

"I love you too, *Alannah*. You are the child of my heart." Nell straightened up, her tone back to normal. "You best get on. You don't want to keep young Cathy and her family waiting."

Kate gave Nell one final hug. She then placed the little bag in her pocket next to the rosary. Without looking back, she left the humble cottage she had lived in for as long as she could remember. She walked down the lane to the crossing where Cathy, Seamus, and Daniel were waiting. Cathy's father Michael was driving the cart. Michael greeted her, his eyes filled with sadness despite his attempt to be cheerful.

"Grand morning, isn't it?"

Kate sniffed back the urge to cry. "Yes, Mr. Madden."

She didn't want to embarrass herself in front of the two lads who took every opportunity to tease her. This morning was different. Daniel jumped down from the back of the cart and took Kate's small bag. He put it on the cart and offered her his hand to help her up to her seat. As she took his hand, he squeezed hers gently. She glanced into his eyes and saw an understanding. She held his gaze for a couple of seconds.

Kate turned to have one last look at her home. Nell wasn't standing outside. A couple of hens pecked at the ground outside the door just as they had every other day. Maisie, the cow swished her tail, as she munched on the dew-covered grass. Kate stifled the urge to run back to the house and hug Nell once more. She gripped the side of the cart as Mr. Madden signaled the horse to move out. Nobody spoke. Kate stared at the thatched cottage until it faded from view. She closed her eyes trying to commit the picture to memory.

Daniel squeezed her hand. "You'll be able to write to her soon. I heard that you can have your picture taken in New York, so you can send that home to her. She'll like that."

"Thank you. You're being kind."

"Don't sound so surprised!" His smile suggested he was teasing. "If I was kind, I wouldn't compare Cathy to a new-born puppy."

Kate put her hand over her mouth to try to stop a

giggle escaping. Cathy was bouncing up and down with excitement. "Cathy's always wanted to go to America." Kate didn't add Cathy wanted to go on the stage.

"Herself and Seamus couldn't be more different. He's so somber and quiet, and Cathy, well, she's great craic."

Kate agreed. Cathy was good fun, most of the time. Seamus never seemed to smile.

"Wonder if he will become a priest. You know, in America."

Daniel stared at Seamus for a couple of seconds. "Maybe, or he could marry the woman of his dreams." Daniel moved closer, his clothes touching Kate's.

She didn't want to be rude, but she didn't want to talk about love and marriage either. "Have you been to Galway city before? I've been once, but it was years ago. I can't remember much about it."

They chatted for a couple of hours before Mr. Madden stopped the cart and suggested lunch.

"Mam had some of the ham left over from the wake," Cathy looked at Daniel. "She thought we might be hungry, so she made a picnic. There's soda bread with ham and some buttermilk."

Kate was amused by Cathy's attempt to flirt with Daniel. Daniel didn't seem interested in anything but the food in front of him.

"She is some woman, your mam." Daniel sank his teeth into his sandwich.

Kate couldn't face food. Her stomach threatened to

heave at any second. She sat on the grass watching Mr. Madden take care of his horses.

Cathy followed Kate's gaze. "Daddy's mad about those horses. Mammy says he treats them better than he does his family."

"Cathy! Your daddy is one of the best men I know. He never took the belt to ye, not like some in our village."

Kate couldn't help but defend Mr. Madden. He was everything she would want in a father.

Cathy sucked in her cheeks. "I know."

Kate's cheeks burned. "Sorry, Cathy. I didn't mean to sound harsh."

"No, you're right. I don't appreciate him. He's always stood up to mammy, too. She gets annoyed with me for running here and there. Daddy always said...he said God made me this way." A tear ran down Cathy's cheek. She brushed it away.

"Go over and talk to him. Bring him a sandwich, and give him a hug. Go on, while you can."

Kate watched as Cathy did as she was bid. Mr. Madden's face lit up with the biggest smile. Kate had to turn away from the tender moment.

It took a few minutes for Cathy and her father to join the rest of them. Mr. Madden put his hand on Kate's shoulder. "Seamus will look after you as well as Cathy, Kate. I promised Nell he would. And a Madden never breaks a promise."

"Seamus can look after Cathy. I will watch Kate." Daniel's comment and tone earned him a look of censure from Mr. Madden. Daniel stiffened, but, before he could respond, Kate spoke up.

"Thank you, Mr. Madden. I'm sure we will all stick together." Kate didn't want an argument to break out. Not today.

CHAPTER 5

*W*hen they reached Galway, they all jumped down, thankful to stretch their legs a bit.

"There's John Burke and his family." Mr. Madden pointed to a group of people. He led Kate and the others over and made the introductions. A small boy stuck his thumb in his mouth, causing Kate to bend down to say hello.

"My name's Kate. What's yours?"

"Sean. I'm five. How old are you?"

Mrs. Burke glared at her son. "Sean Burke! I am sorry, Kate. He is a bit overwhelmed. I hope you don't mind us calling you, Kate."

"Not at all, Margaret. Are you ready to leave?" Immediately Kate regretted speaking. Margaret's eyes glistened with unshed tears, as she looked back toward the city.

"John says it will be the making of us. Lots of opportunity in America for the children," Margaret said.

Kate glanced at the girls clutching their mother's skirts. They didn't seem keen to go either. Not that it mattered. If the man of the house wanted to leave Ireland, his family followed him. Mr. Burke's animated tone suggested he was as excited as Cathy.

Sean pulled at Kate's hand. "Do you know the ship is bigger than a city? Imagine that, Kate. It's so big it takes you two days to get from one end to the other."

"Sean Burke, don't be telling stories. It is big, but not that huge. Now mind your manners, lad. Kate doesn't want to be putting up with you running around her like a mad dog."

"Sorry, Mammy, I'm a bit excited."

"You are, my darling boy," Mrs. Burke responded, ruffling his hair and giving him a kiss. Kate looked on, amused at Sean's response to his mother. He pushed his hair back into place and moved closer to his father, clearly trying to be like the man of the house. His two sisters looked overawed by what was going on and clung onto their rag dolls. Kate smiled at them, hoping to make them feel a little better.

Mr. Burke had brought a horse and cart and was planning on selling them when they arrived in Athlone. From there they would take the train. Cathy's father had paid Burke a few shillings to take his son, daughter, and their two friends. Kate was relieved. It was faster and slightly more comfortable than walking.

She bowed her head, as Cathy and Seamus said

goodbye to their father. A small crowd had gathered to wish the Burkes good luck.

"It's a big adventure you are off on now, lad," a man said to Daniel. "Is that the wife going with you? Fine looking woman."

Kate blushed, as Daniel took her hand and said, "She is, isn't she?"

As the cart, piled high with the family's trunks and their bags, drove out of the town, the well-wishers waved them off.

Kate tucked her hand back into her skirts. She looked up to catch Daniel grinning at her.

"Sorry about that, Kate, but I couldn't resist. And he was right. You are a fine-looking woman."

Kate didn't reply. Was what Cathy'd told her true? Was Daniel fond of her? Realizing she was staring, she looked down. Her breath caught when he took her hand. She risked glancing up, but he was looking back toward the city. He was a tall man, his broad shoulders almost blocking her view. His calloused hands were gentle. Her skin tingled, as he rubbed his thumb up and down hers.

She caught Cathy's knowing look, her friend's eyes dropping pointedly to Kate's hands. Face flushing, Kate pulled her hand away and used it to pull the collar of her dress free from her neck. Was it her imagination, or had the weather become warmer?

She sensed Daniel look at her. She didn't move a muscle. He didn't try to take her hand in his. Instead of being relieved, her stomach clenched with disappointment.

CHAPTER 6

*D*elia Furlong picked at a loose thread on her gown. This was it. In less than ten minutes she would be married. In her dreams, she had imagined a full church with people she loved wishing Conor and her a wonderful life together. She never guessed she'd elope, but her aunt had left her no choice.

She told herself she didn't care there was nobody here save Cook, Mrs. Fitzgerald, and Conor's mother, who acted as the witnesses.

"Are you sure this is what you want, Delia?"

"Yes, Father Andreas."

The priest nodded and began the service. Father Andreas may not have believed Delia, if Lady Fitzgerald hadn't been so forthright in her views on Aunt Cecilia and her plans for Delia. The ceremony was over very quickly, and the four of them went to a small café for tea and cake paid for by Lady Fitzgerald. Cook had to get back to Aunt Cecilia's house before she was missed.

Delia hugged the large woman close, their tears mingling as they said goodbye. This kind-hearted woman had saved Delia on numerous occasions from the wrath of her aunt and made her miserable existence as happy as she could.

Cook handed Delia a present and clasped her hand.

"You be happy now Miss Delia and forget all about the mistress. You have a good man in Conor Brennan." Cook left as quickly as her little legs would take her.

Delia stared at her retreating figure until the woman disappeared from view. Then she opened her hand to find a five-pound note stuffed inside. "Dear Cook, she was always so kind to me."

"I wonder if she will finally come and work for me now that you've gone. She is easily the best cook in Dublin. I don't know why she stuck with your aunt for so long," Lady Fitzgerald said. "She used to make your mother and me the most delicious cakes, when we were younger."

Delia's mouth watered at the thought of Cook's baking. "She stayed because of me. She protected me. Said it was because she loved my mother so much. I do hope she doesn't get into trouble with Aunt Cecilia. I don't trust that woman."

"I will look after Cook, don't you fret, Delia. Now, let me look at you, a married woman! Your mother would have been so proud of you." Lady Fitzgerald hugged Delia, her eyes glistening. "Your father, too, I'm sure."

Delia hugged her mother's friend back. "Thank you, Lady Fitz- I mean Geraldine. If it wasn't for you, I would never have gotten away from Aunt Cecilia. You convinced her to allow me to accompany you."

"Cecilia is a silly woman. She actually believed your proposed engagement to that pompous reverend somehow elevated your social status."

Delia thought she saw amusement in Geraldine's expression, but she didn't know her well enough to be sure.

"Let's get going. Your train won't wait for you." Geraldine turned to Conor's mam. "Mrs. Brennan, why don't you sit beside me in my cab? Conor and Delia can share the seat opposite."

Poor Mrs. Brennan almost curtsied to Lady Fitzpatrick. Delia nudged Conor to help his mother into the cab. He assisted Geraldine, too, charming the older woman with his smile. Then he turned to his bride.

Conor's hands lingered at her waist a few seconds too long. Heat rushed to her cheeks, as he kissed her before helping her into the cab.

THE FOURSOME TRAVELED to the train station to see the young couple off. Conor's mam cried buckets, and even Mrs. Fitzgerald dabbed her eyes.

"Look at us, all married now. How are you feeling Mrs. Brennan?" Conor asked, causing Delia to look at his mother. A nudge from Conor set her straight, as Mrs. Brennan and Geraldine exchanged amused glances.

"We are having a honeymoon in style, nothing but

the best for my wife. A trip on the RMS *Titanic* no less. We sail tomorrow afternoon."

The newspapers had been full of stories about the *Titanic* and its maiden voyage. Conor had kept copies of all of them for Delia to read on the train. No ship had been built like it.

"My word, but I am jealous. The Astor's and other famous people are traveling on her. I asked my husband to buy tickets, but he said he was too busy at work. Delia, darling, you will have a wonderful time." Geraldine kissed her on the cheek, but Delia was still staring at Conor.

"We don't sail until tomorrow." Delia bit her lip. "Aunt Cecilia may track us down." Delia hated lowering the mood, but she was worried about her aunt. She wouldn't put anything past the woman.

"Darling, nobody is going to part us," Conor took her face gently in his hands, pressing his lips against hers. "I promise you. Put a smile on your face, and say goodbye to everyone."

Delia did as she was bid, promising Conor's mam she would make him write home once they got to New York. She also promised to write to Lady Fitzgerald.

"Live a long and happy life, Delia darling. Your parents would want that for you." Geraldine pushed a small bag into Delia's hands.

Delia protested. "You gave us a gift already. You bought my clothes."

"You can't go to a new country without having a nest egg. It's only a small amount. By rights, you should have an inheritance from your grandfather. He was rich enough. Off you go, and don't think about the past. You have found yourself a fine young man."

Lady Fitzgerald held out her hand to Conor.

"Thank you again for everything, Mrs. Fitzgerald. I will look after my wife," Conor said, proudly shaking the woman's hand.

Delia liked the sound of that. His wife.

CHAPTER 7

WEDNESDAY, APRIL 10TH,
SOUTHAMPTON

Gerry Walker shut the door of the house behind him, as he set off on the walk to the docks. Passing a pillar box, he dropped in a letter to his mam back in Ireland.

He shivered, as he pulled his jacket closed, thankful it wasn't raining. As he marched down in the direction of the port, he passed a number of the brewery houses. No doubt his mates were still inside taking advantage of their last few hours of freedom. They had heard the work on the *Titanic* would be easier than that involved on older ships, but they would still be in the belly of the ship for most of the duration, facing the melting pots of the boilers.

He patted his pocket to check that his money was still there. He planned on buying Jean a ring in New York and making an honest woman of her, when he came back from this trip. He closed his eyes, picturing her smile. She was a wonderful woman, and he was the luckiest man alive. He had money set aside for their new home in Southampton, a house near where her mother lived. Her mother would keep Jean company, when he was at sea, and help her with the children, assuming they were blessed.

A stoker friend had a mate who knew someone selling jewelry in New York and had promised all the gang a good price. He was bound to be getting a cut of the business, but Gerry didn't care. Jean was a great girl, understanding about his being away at sea for weeks on end. She understood better than most, having a brother, Tommy, who also worked on the ships. Tommy was a steward and had been promoted to First Class for this trip. Gerry knew they wouldn't see much of each other, the *Titanic* being such a large ship, but they'd go for a few drinks in New York.

"Irish, you are coming in for the last pint, lad?"

Gerry turned at the sound of his nickname, the lads had given it to him for his shock of red hair. Jackson grinned out of the window of the public house. He was always late onto the ships, but he got away with it, due in part to his large size and his reputation for being good at his job.

"Not today, Jackson, got to be on time for the new ship."

"Come on, Irish, I'll stand you a whiskey."

Tempted, Gerry was about to join them when he spotted more of the stokers up ahead of him.

"Next time, Jackson, I got to see a man about a piece of gold."

"Under the thumb already, lad, there's no saving you now," Jackson teased in his way. "Catch up with you later," He shouted and disappeared.

Gerry strode, increasing his pace until he caught up with some other lads from the ship. They traded stories of their time ashore, as they made their way to the docks.

"Jesus, Mary and Joseph, would you look at the size of her! We'll never be able to find our way back out of her once we get on board." The stoker rubbed his beard, as they all stared at the ship.

"I thought there would be fanfares and such like." The speaker sounded disappointed. "It's her first trip, after all."

"All that happened in Belfast. You know what those Paddies are like for their parties," another man said. He shot a grin at Gerry.

Gerry paid no attention to the teasing, he knew it was par for the course and not meant in a bad way. They nodded at the Sixth Officer, Moody, as they walked up the gangway, their papers having been checked thoroughly and, with one last look at the sky, went below.

"Where're our berths?" Gerry asked someone who seemed to know where he was going. The ship was so big he could well imagine getting lost.

"We're staying in First Class, Irish. Didn't you hear?" one of the stokers teased him.

"As if. The black gang is always in the bottom. You couldn't possibly risk upsetting someone's little princess by bumping into them, could you?" another man said.

"I know what I'd like to do to some of those women

in the First Class. Do you see their clothes and skin? They look so soft and -"

"That's enough out of you. Show some respect for your betters," an officer reprimanded the fireman. Firemen, greasers, and trimmers are quartered in the bow." The officer cleared his throat. "D through G deck – go down there," the officer pointed at a companionway, "you'll find it eventually. If you land in the sea you have gone too far."

Gerry followed his advice, hoping the man hadn't been making fun of him and his friends. Tensions were high on the docks due to the coal strike. Thousands were out of work. Gerry and his colleagues were lucky to get work on the *Titanic*. There were some who felt only British crew members should be on board, not Irish Catholics. He hoped his chief wasn't one of them.

But the directions were good, and he found his bed in a cabin filled with the rest of the crew.

"Not much room to swing a cat in here, eh, Gerry?"

"Did you bring a cat?"

"I was just saying," the Scottish hand responded, but Gerry was already on his way out the door. He had to report for the first shift.

About noon, the whistle blew for friends of those traveling to go ashore.

"Won't be long now," Fireman Barrett said to his crew. "Get those furnaces nice and hot."

"Yes, sir." The men responded as one.

Gerry shoveled the coal faster. Barrett would pick up a shovel and help, if needed.

"Did you hear he's taken a berth with the rest of us?" one of the stokers said.

Gerry shook his head. The man didn't take the hint.

"I like him. He's still one of us even though he's a leading fireman. Cares about us, he does. Probably why the senior officers aren't too fond of him."

Gerry didn't reply not wanting to get involved in gossip. He was saved by the arrival of a late crew member.

"Jackson and his gang can't get on; that bloomin' Sixth Officer, Moody won't let them. I think his uniform has gone to his head," one of the men came rushing down the stairs heading for Barrett.

"Slow down man, you aren't making any sense," Barrett replied.

"Sorry, sir. I just got on meself, and then I heard shouts behind me. Jackson and the rest of the lads came running up behind me with their kitbags slung over their shoulders, but he, the Sixth Officer, said they were too late. He'd already pulled up the gangway. I heard Jackson shouting at him, but, even then, he refused to move."

Jackson, being such a large man, rarely had to raise his voice in order to get anyone to allow him to do anything.

"What happened?" Barrett asked.

"They left Jackson and the rest of the lads on shore. What will they do now?"

"Find another ship is my guess. Jackson won't want to go home to his missus. She'll kill him. Five kids to feed and another on the way," Gerry said. Those around him nodded. Mrs. Jackson's temper was legendary, with Jackson himself using her as the reason he spent so much time at sea.

"He must be gutted. Wouldn't want to miss this trip, would you Gerry?" one of the crew asked, "They will be talking about this in the history books, you mark my words. A ship this big has never sailed before."

"Lads stop hanging around like a bevy of women after church. We got work to do," Barrett shouted.

"What about the missing crew members?"

"We can pick up more at Queenstown, if they are needed. Backs into it now, lads. We don't want any more trouble today," Barrett replied.

Warning bells rang almost immediately.

"What the blazes is wrong now?" someone shouted.

There was no answer, just a series of orders from Barrett. Nobody spoke until they were out to sea.

"What happened when we left the dock?" Davy asked Barrett, who'd just come back down below.

Barret spoke through clenched teeth. "We almost collided with the SS *New York*."

Gerry and the rest of the gang stared at their chief. Barrett didn't look concerned.

"Forget it, lads. No harm done."

"Chief, how did that happen?"

"Nothing happened, Davy, thanks to the quick actions of officers and crew on both ships. Get back to work." Barrett walked away.

The men exchanged glances. A number crossed

themselves. One spat on the floor. "A near collision is a bad omen for this voyage."

A few of the men nodded in response to the man's comment.

They'll be going on about tea leaves and banshees next. Gerry knew seamen were superstitious, but they were making something out of nothing. "Stop behaving like a bunch of superstitious old women. You heard the chief. We've work to do."

Gerry resumed shoveling, and, after a few seconds of griping, the men around him followed suit.

CHAPTER 8

WEDNESDAY, APRIL 10TH, DUBLIN

*D*elia gripped Conor's arm, as they tried to find the platform for the Queenstown train. The noise was deafening, the shrill whistles from guardsmen combatting with the chatter from the crowds of people gathered on every platform.

Conor's tall, broad shoulders protected her from being buffeted by people desperate to secure their travel.

"I'm glad I purchased the tickets in advance. Just look at those queues."

Delia didn't respond, not that he would have heard her over the noise.

"There's our train. Come on, love. We don't have much time." Conor pulled her along with him. Delia had to run a little to keep up with his long strides.

It took a couple of minutes to find their seats. Delia sat next to the window with Conor beside her. Her husband stored their cases on the rack above their heads.

A couple of men sat down opposite them. "Afternoon, missus. The name's John Taylor, and this is my brother, Brian. Are you traveling the whole way?"

Conor took Delia's arm and tucked it into his. "Conor Brennan and my wife, Delia. We are heading to America on the Titanic."

Delia smiled to herself, hearing the pride in her husband's voice. The Taylors grew more animated, and soon the men were discussing the ship. Bored with the details, Delia gazed out the window. Her eyes kept closing, the sleepless night catching up with her.

Conor nudged her. "Wake up, darling. We're here."

Delia clung to Conor, as the crowds of people threatened to overwhelm her.

"Do you know how to get to the hotel?"

"No. We will take a cab."

Delia didn't argue. Too tired to fight her way through the crowds, she was relieved to be traveling in style. The journey didn't take long. Soon the cabbie pulled up in front of a luxurious hotel.

Delia spoke softly, so the driver wouldn't hear her. "Conor, he must be mistaken. We can't afford this."

"No mistake, Delia. Have you got your bag?"

Delia showed him her bag, her eyes on the luxurious hotel. A doorman held the door while another took their bags from Conor.

"Stop worrying and enjoy yourself. Lady Fitzgerald wanted to surprise you."

"Oh, she is such a dear lady," Delia said, as she surveyed the hotel. "She must have known rooms were going for premium rates. The whole of Ireland seems to have descended on Cobh. All these people can't be traveling on the *Titanic*. Can they?"

The desk clerk looked up. "No, missus. We have a number of guests who only wish to see the ship for themselves. Our hotel will be empty again by Thursday. You benefited from the last available room."

"Thank you," Delia said. She glanced around her as Conor signed the register. Her feet sank into the carpet, as she walked over to admire the flower arrangement sitting pride of place beside the front counter. She spotted a painting of Cobh Harbor on the wall. She turned to point it out to Conor, but he was in conversation with the desk clerk. Tired, Delia decided to sit down. Conor found her almost asleep.

"You can have a lie down, if you like? Our room is ready."

"I don't want to miss a tiny detail of our trip. This place is amazing. Look at that painting."

"Mrs. Fitzgerald said it would be best to hide in plain sight. Your aunt won't think of looking for us here, I mean, if she does find out," Conor explained. His eyes looked everywhere but at her.

The hair on the back of her neck rose. "What aren't you telling me?"

"Let's go to our room, and I will explain." Conor glanced toward the desk clerk who turned bright red. He had clearly been eavesdropping. The bell boy picked up their cases and led the way to their rooms. Conor tipped him a couple of coins, making Delia smile. Conor acted as if he stayed in nice hotels every day, rather than this being his first time.

When the bell boy had gone, Conor closed the door and led Delia to sit on the bed. He held her hand.

"There was a telegram at the front desk. Mrs. Fitzgerald sent it. Somehow your aunt found out we ran away together. She has sent someone to Southampton to bring you home."

"She can't force me to come back."

"She can, if she sends an armed man after you."

"She wouldn't."

But, even as she said the words, Delia knew her aunt would stop at nothing to get her own way. Conor put his arms around her, as she gave way to shuddering sobs. She couldn't wait to get on the *Titanic* and get away from her aunt's hatred.

"Delia Brennan, I promise you, your aunt can't hurt you now. We will soon be on the other side of the world. Too far away even for her to cause us any harm. Now come here, wife, and kiss me."

She caught the look in his eyes, his passion for her making her heart beat faster. Closing her eyes, she raised her face for his kiss. He was right. They were married now, and nothing was going to tear them apart.

They didn't leave the room for fear, Conor said, someone would recognize them.

"Sure, who would know us down here in Queenstown?" she teased him, knowing right well why he wanted to stay indoors.

He nuzzled the side of her neck. "You never know, wife. It pays to be careful you know."

They ordered room service, and, for the next few hours, it was as if only the two of them mattered. Then came morning and the day for sailing.

"Come on, darling, wake up and get dressed. Our ship awaits." Conor kissed her on the nose. "I am going downstairs to get the paper. I will be back shortly to escort you to our home for the next week. Imagine, Delia, in seven days' time we will be in America."

Delia just smiled. She didn't care where they went so long as they were together. She thought she loved him before they got married, but now she couldn't imagine ever living without him. For the first time, she could honestly say she understood her mother leaving everything behind for her da. She pitied her aunt for never having felt this way about anyone.

The crowds moving toward the dock area were daunting. It seemed like everyone in Ireland was traveling. She held tight to Conor's hand, as they moved forward, and soon they were on the tender taking them to RMS *Titanic*, anchored at the mouth of the harbor. It was bigger than anything she had ever seen, the four black funnels set against the clear sky.

"It would take a week to walk around the ship for sure," she said to Conor.

"I heard it took some of the officers up to two weeks to learn all the shortcuts on board." Conor looked up at it. "There was a fella in the hotel who said there was a priest who traveled over from Southampton, took a lot of pictures of it. He's been offered a fortune for them from the newspapers."

"Why are all the lifeboats on that part of the ship?" Delia pointed to the boat deck. She only spotted the crew member after she spoke.

"We're unsinkable, missus. Don't be worrying your pretty little head about no lifeboats."

He moved away before Delia could respond. She stared out at the ocean. Conor put his arm around her waist. Delia leaned into his body. She couldn't speak. She was torn. Much as she never wanted to see her aunt again, Ireland was her home. It was hard saying goodbye.

CHAPTER 9

THURSDAY, APRIL 11TH, QUEENSTOWN, CORK

*F*inally, after a long train journey, Kate, Cathy, and their party arrived in Queenstown. It was after noon when the *Titanic* arrived putting down anchor at the harbor mouth. She was every bit as huge as the men had said she'd be, too big to come right into the dock. To Kate, the ship looked like a big island.

Daniel's eyes widened, as he stared at the *Titanic*. "Isn't she the most beautiful thing you ever saw?"

Kate didn't comment. She wanted to turn and run back to Granny Nell. She had a horrible feeling about this ship, her mind going back to the peddler woman who had told their fortunes at the fair last summer. She had read the tea leaves and told Cathy and herself, a great tragedy would befall them. But, when they had pressed for details, the woman had crossed herself, had refused payment, and, to the astonishment of the crowd waiting to hear their fortunes, had refused to read any more leaves. Nell had dismissed her as a fraud, but Kate wasn't too sure. She'd seen the look of terror in the woman's eyes. Nobody was that good an actor. Shivering, she pulled her shawl tighter around her shoulders.

"Isn't it great they provide the meals onboard. If we had gone on another ship, we would have had to bring our own food."

Kate didn't reply to Daniel's running commentary. She guessed he didn't need her to, as he didn't stop talking. Maybe he was nervous, too, and this was his way of hiding it. She glanced at his face, but his eyes were bright, full of excitement. She looked away not wanting him to see the fear in hers.

Then someone in the crowd screamed. She took a step back, but Daniel grabbed her hand. She had seen it, too. A head appeared out of one of the ship's four funnels.

"'Tis nothing, Kate. Some eejit of a crew member trying to frighten us, is all," he whispered close to her ear. She barely heard him over the roars of the crowd. She had never seen anything like it. The whole of County Cork seemed to have gathered to see the *Titanic*. Surely all these people couldn't be sailing. There wouldn't be any room on the ship for everyone.

"Come on," Daniel said. "The tenders won't wait."

Kate stared at Daniel in horror. She didn't want to travel in a small boat. There were two of them, called *PS America* and *PS Ireland*. A lad, she later learned was named Eugene Daly, played the pipes, as the tender sailed out to it. The crowd at the jetty sang along to the rebel song, a *Nation Once*

Again. Kate glanced up, spotting the stony face of an *RMS Titanic* officer. His expression suggested he didn't care for their choice of song. She opened her mouth and joined in. Ireland was her home, and this was the last time she would see it. So, what if an *Englishman* didn't like their singing about the time when Ireland would belong to the Irish?

"'Tis an awful racket he be making. The officers won't like it. Do you see their reaction?"

Kate turned to see who was talking and found a middle-aged woman staring back at her. The woman looked at Kate, as if she was something she had trodden on. Kate found herself looking down at her clothes to make sure there wasn't a lump of mud or a batch of hay making her look dirty. When she looked up again, the woman was giving another lady the same evil looks.

"Maybe she is on the run. Looks like she could have done time in the Joy, doesn't she?"

Kate laughed despite Daniel's comment being rude. She couldn't imagine the prim and proper woman spending time visiting someone in Dublin's notorious jail, never mind being an inmate.

"That's better. Never let anyone rob you of your smile, Kate Maloney. It lights up the world."

Embarrassed, she couldn't look at him but stared over his shoulder at the sea view. She joined back in with the singing, his support making her feel better. A large wave hit the tender and put a stop to her singing.

Daniel brushed the hair out of Kate's eyes. "It's safe, Kate. Just hold on tight and you will soon be in the lap of luxury. You can hold my hand and close your eyes if you want."

She looked away from the warm expression in his eyes. When she glanced back, he was still staring at her.

"We got to stick together, now. Cathy and Seamus have each other, the Burkes are family, so that leaves us."

She smiled, as she took his hand. When he put it like that, how could she refuse?

CHAPTER 10

*K*ate's heart beat faster, as they approached the huge ship that towered out of the water. It was as big as a city. They followed the steerage passengers. All of them had to be examined by the ship's doctor. Kate stood in silence, as the ship's doctor pulled at her eyelids. He said something about checking for some eye disease she had never heard of. Cathy whispered he would be able to see white scars on their eyelids if they had it, and then they would be sent home. They both passed the test and so did the boys. The stewards directed them where to go. The cabins for single women were at one end of the ship, and the men were at the other. The girls were sharing a cabin with some other passengers, all female obviously.

Seamus grabbed Daniel's arm. "Come on. Let's find our own cabin."

Daniel turned to look at Kate, "I will find you for

dinner. Now put a smile on your face, and don't go running off with any sailor."

Kate and Cathy stood watching until the men disappeared from view. Lifting their cases, they exchanged smiles.

"This is such an adventure, Kate. We have to remember every detail. Mam and Nell will want to hear all about it."

"How do we know where to go? Every passageway looks exactly the same." Kate clutched her bag to her side. She wasn't at all sure she'd be able to find her way back up top. Finally, just as she was about to declare they were lost, they reached their cabin. Cathy pushed the door open. "Oh, my goodness, will you look at this. It's beautiful."

Cathy threw her bag on the bottom bunk. "Kate, you take the top one. This is traveling in luxury, so it is."

Kate nodded. She couldn't find her voice. The cabin, while small, was luxurious compared to what she was used to.

Cathy moved to the electric light switch. "It works just like they have at the big house. Do you see?"

Kate figured that was a rhetorical question. She looked at the wash basin, but Cathy beat her to it and turned on the taps.

"Wish I could see what the cabins are like in First Class, if we have these luxuries. Can you imagine, Kate?"

Kate shook her head, she couldn't believe their luck. She sat on her bed feeling the mattress beneath her.

"Cathy, try the mattress. It's so soft. Look at the blankets and pillows. They have the name of the ship on them." Kate fingered the bed linen. "Nell was right to tell us to pack sheets."

Kate pulled out the sheets from her luggage and soon had the bed made to her satisfaction. "We'll sleep like babies."

Cathy finished her bed. "I think coming on the RMS *Titanic* was the best decision we ever made. Let's dump our things here and go exploring?"

Kate was only too keen to agree. She put her bags on her bed but kept the clay and the rosary beads in the pocket of her skirt. She didn't want to lose the precious mementos.

"Do you want to go up top to wave goodbye?" Kate asked Cathy, as they walked through the Third Class area, Kate following Cathy, amazed her friend knew where to go.

"But we don't know anyone," Cathy said, her tone suggesting she'd prefer to explore their new surroundings.

"I know that, but it will be our last time to see Ireland for a while. You can stay here, if you like, but I'm going." Kate sounded braver than she felt. She wanted to go up on deck but not alone.

"Ah, sure I will. I want to be able to tell my grandchildren all about this voyage." Cathy hugged herself. "Aren't we the lucky ones, Kate. We are traveling in style, sure we are."

Kate didn't answer. She was too busy staring in awe at the coastline. She could barely see the sheer granite cliffs, her eyesight blurred by tears. She coughed to clear her scratchy throat. Brushing a tear away, she knew she needed a distraction or she would dissolve into a blubbering mess.

"Cathy, what's caviar?"

"Fish eggs. Why?"

"I heard one of the sailors moaning about the number of crates of champagne and boxes of caviar on board."

"Champagne! Wish we had some down here. It's lovely." Cathy turned away from the view to look at Kate. "Not that I've tasted it, not yet. Mam told me about the parties at the big house. They had champagne all the time, and once the master sent some to the staff to drink on New Year's Eve. Mam said it was very bubbly."

Seamus came up behind Cathy and pinched her waist, causing her to squeal. Kate laughed at the furious expression on Cathy's face, as she turned on her brother.

"Seamus Madden, will you behave."

Seamus shrugged his shoulders. Daniel gave him a playful punch.

"Cathy, I apologize on his behalf. Have you girls seen the place we eat?"

"Daniel, it's the dining saloon, if you please," Seamus said, taking his hat off his head and pretending to be posh.

"It looks even better than it did in that picture I left with my mam." Daniel barely took a breath before continuing, "It's situated two decks under the First Class dining area. We get three meals a day, but you have to be quick. It only has places for about four hundred people."

Four hundred? How many people were traveling on this ship? Kate didn't want to ask for fear of sounding stupid.

"You're a big eejit, Donnelly. They are going to have two sittings." Cathy poked Daniel in the arm.

Daniel threw his eyes up to heaven, making Kate smile at his antics. She guessed he'd probably known about the eating plans all along but was trying to amuse them.

"There's a swimming pool on board, too, but we're not allowed to use it. It's only for the rich lot." Daniel's comment was met with silence.

Kate couldn't swim, so she wasn't at all concerned about missing out.

Time passed slowly. Someone said they had to wait for the mail to be loaded. Some enterprising Irish ladies had joined the ship in a bid to sell some of their lace to the First Class passengers. Almost two hours passed before the liner raised the anchor. It was shortly after 1:30pm.

Kate gazed back out to shore, most everyone around them falling quiet, as the big ship sailed past the coast of Ireland.

"It'll be a long time before we see her again, won't it?" Daniel whispered to Kate. "But don't fret, darling girl, when you have made a fortune in America, you can come back and show everyone just who Kate Maloney is. You might even sail back in First Class and have a go in the pool. I'd join you, but it seems they like to keep the men and women separate."

Kate blushed at his flirting, but, instead of being annoyed, she was comforted. She sensed he was feeling rather lonely, too.

CHAPTER 11

*G*erry and his mate, Davy, snuck up on deck for a last look at home before the ship left Queenstown. Keeping a lookout for officers or stewards who would report them to the chief, Gerry made a mental promise to go home to see his mother the next time he got to Southampton.

"When were you last home to see your mam?" Davy asked, as they both stared at the harbor and watched the little tenders coming alongside.

"The best part of two years. Mam understands I've been saving to get wed."

"An English girl, is she?"

"Yes. Her brother works as a steward, been promoted to First Class."

"My brother is an engineer. Doubt I'll see much of him this trip though. It's his first job since university, so he won't want to be seen with the likes of me." Davy smiled, as he glanced down at his coal dust covered clothes.

"Gerry, what are you doing on deck? Chief will kill you."

Tommy's voice nearly gave Gerry a heart attack, as he hadn't seen the man coming. But he pretended not to be worried.

"What he doesn't know can't hurt him." Gerry gave the steward a hearty clap on his back. "What's the craic with you, Tommy?"

"I'll leave you two alone. I'll catch you later, Gerry," Davy said.

Given their respective roles, Gerry and Tommy, his soon-to-be brother-in-law, didn't socialize on the ship but often saw each other back in Southampton.

"I have some lovely passengers to look after. This is one of them. I have to take it for a walk." Tommy looked at the dog nipping at his heels, his sarcasm evident.

Gerry bent down to pat the dog's head. He loved animals of all types, and usually they returned the favor, but not this one. He got a nip for his troubles.

"Yeah, she's as temperamental as her owner, but don't tell anyone I said that. I best be getting back. You should go, too," Tommy said, "Don't want to start the trip on the wrong side of your chief."

"Yes, Tommy, lad, I won't get into trouble, I promise."

With a last look at the Irish mountains and a gulp of

fresh air, Gerry made his way back to the bowels of the ship. He would be back on duty before anyone missed him.

He was barely back at his station when Davy came over, his eyes wide.

"Chief, there's a fire in the coal in boiler room six, must have been going on since the ship left Belfast. I need help to dig it out."

Barrett nodded. "Gerry, get a team to dig that out. It's the cheap coal brought in due to the blasted coal strike."

"Yes, sir." Gerry joined the twelve-man team digging out the coal to get the fire out.

CHAPTER 12

*D*elia's stomach swirled, as she struggled not to be sick. The short journey on the tender from the quayside to the ship was enough to put her off taking an ocean voyage. She hadn't understood the steward's directions. What did he mean by starboard? She breathed deeply, trying not to think about the sea.

Conor set her on her feet, having insisted on carrying her over the threshold of their cabin.

"Feeling better, darling?"

Delia held her stomach, as she took a step. It was just like walking in the hotel. The floor didn't lurch as the awful tender had.

Conor put his arms around her, his cheek resting on her head. "You would hardly know you were at sea."

She turned to embrace him. "I don't think I will ever get tired of having your arms around me. You make me feel safe and loved. I want you to hold me forever." She reached up to kiss him. His arms drew her closer, as he deepened the kiss. Leaving her slightly breathless, he dropped a kiss on her hair.

"Do you fancy going up on top to say goodbye to the homeland?"

She didn't, but she knew he wanted to. So, she nodded, determined not to make her husband unhappy. Together they made their way to the Third Class deck area.

"Conor, what did the steward mean when he said starboard?"

"You have to speak sailor's language now, Delia. No such thing as left and right. Instead it's port and starboard. Our cabin is on the right side."

"Why couldn't he just say that?"

Conor kissed the top of her head. "He did, darling."

He smiled, as she poked him in the ribs for being cheeky. Holding her by the hand, he drew her forward to the rail.

She didn't want to look at the sea. She concentrated on the view far away on shore.

"Look at those farm houses. They look tiny from here. The fields look so green, don't they? They have a lovely view of those mountains. Must be a nice place to live."

"Delia Brennan, are you telling me you want to be a farmer's wife."

Delia snuggled into his side. "I'm happy as your wife.

He put his arms around her waist. "Will you miss it?"

His question brought her aunt to mind. As quick as the thought arrived, she dismissed it. That woman wasn't going to ruin her life. "Not while I am with you. You are all I need, Conor Brennan."

She turned so she was facing her husband. The crisp afternoon air blew strands of her hair into her eyes. She brushed them aside. "Aunt Cecilia is a lunatic. I don't know if she was serious when she threatened us. I'm glad we are on our way. She can't hurt us now."

His lips brushed against hers. "Delia, as long as I live, nobody will hurt you again."

Together they stared at the coastline, as their view changed from green fields to granite cliffs. Delia couldn't believe she didn't feel seasick.

"It's like the field is moving. I can't even feel anything. We are moving, aren't we?"

"Look down there, Delia. See how the water is turning darker. That's the motion of the engines swirling up the sand."

All dread of being confined to her quarters by seasickness fled. Instead, she was filled with excitement and a sense of opportunity. She kissed her husband firmly on the lips. Conor grinned.

"What was that for?"

"I love you, and I can't wait for our new life to start in America. It will be wonderful."

"I love you, too, Mrs. Brennan. Would you like to explore our new quarters for a while?"

Giggling, as he waggled his eyebrows at her, she took his hand and let him lead her back the way they had come. There would be plenty of time later to explore this wonderful ship and meet other people who were also going to America, the land of Dreams.

CHAPTER 13

Kate and Cathy held hands, as they stared at the Irish coastline. Despite her talk about not looking back, Cathy was crying. Kate couldn't reassure her friend. She hated leaving home, and watching her country disappear was torture.

"Next time, we will sail into Queenstown in First Class," Daniel said.

Nobody disagreed with him. Kate was too choked up to comment.

"There you are, lads and lassies. Been looking all over for ye. Did you get settled into your accommodation? There's a big hall for us to have a dance in later." Mr. Burke barely had the words said when they heard the plaintive tones of the uilleann pipes.

"That's Eugene Daly. He's wearing his kilt and playing the Irish bagpipes. He's a great player. He was telling me at the harbor, he's on his way to a Gaelic Festival in Celtic Park, Queens, New York. He's traveling with his sister and a friend. He invited us to come to see him play on May nineteenth. He could wrench a tear from a stone creature with the way he plays those pipes. Brings a tear to my eye, I don't mind telling you that."

Kate couldn't comment, as she found herself overcome, too.

Cathy took Kate by the hand. "Come on, let's get downstairs and unpack. We'll see you, boys, later."

"Thanks, Cathy. I said I wouldn't cry anymore, and yet I can't stop blubbering like a baby."

"Sure, I am the same myself." Cathy wiped a tear away. "I want to go to America, I really do. Now we are leaving, it seems so final. I think everyone is feeling a bit emotional, even Seamus."

Kate didn't think Cathy's solemn brother would cry over anything but decided it was best not to comment.

When Kate and Cathy returned to their cabin, they met the other ladies they would be sharing with. Kate's heart sank a little. She recognized one of them as the opinionated lady Daniel had suggested was running from prison. The other woman held her hand out. She spoke with a cork accent.

"Name's Eileen Murphy."

Kate shook the woman's hand. Eileen looked to be in her late twenties.

"My name's Kate Maloney, and this is my friend, Cathy Madden." Kate held out her hand to the other woman, waiting for her to identify herself.

"Mary Ryan."

Kate shook Mary's hand. Kate got the impression from the way the woman was looking at Cathy and her, they didn't meet with her approval. Kate attempted to warm the chilly atmosphere.

"Our cabin is lovely, isn't it?"

Mary's lip curled, but Kate ignored her.

"Have you been to America before, Mary?"

"No, I have not. I should be on my way to England, only, my poor mistress took ill and died. Her family thought the world of me. They arranged my new position. I am to be a lady's maid, but that is all I can say. Discretion is my middle name."

Kate couldn't look at Cathy for fear she would laugh. Could Mary hear herself?

"What about you, Eileen? Have you been to America?"

"Yes, I emigrated some ten years ago. I came home as mammy wanted to make my wedding dress using Irish lace. Andrew, he's my fiancé, is a store owner in Chicago."

Mary sniffed, causing Eileen to blush and look at her shoes. Kate could have slapped Mary for putting the other woman down. Kate was thinking of a good reply, but Cathy beat her to it.

"A store owner, how exciting. You will never want for anything. I'm going on the stage," Cathy said.

Kate thought Mary was going to be ill. Her face was the color of the linen sheets. She coughed and made her excuses. Once the door closed behind Mary, the atmosphere in the cabin lightened considerably. Cathy started to laugh, and soon Kate and Eileen had joined in.

After a couple of seconds, Eileen covered her mouth. She glanced at the other girls.

"I shouldn't be laughing. It's not kind." Eileen took a deep breath. "Mary is just very annoying."

"True. I wonder why she's really going to America." Kate mused. "Eileen, it must have been hard for your mammy to miss your wedding."

"It was. Andrew wrote to Daddy to tell him he would look after me. He also helped me pay for Callum, my younger brother to go to the seminary in Maynooth. Mammy was happy."

Cathy looked up, her expression suitably impressed. Kate had to look away. She knew Cathy couldn't care less about someone becoming a priest.

"What a lovely thing to do, Eileen. Maynooth turns out the best priests in Ireland. That was kind of both of you."

Kate bit her lip. Cathy sounded so sincere. Maybe she did belong on the stage.

Eileen flicked a thread off her dress. "It's every Irish mammy's dream to have a son in the priesthood." Eileen picked up her Bible and began to read.

Kate and Cathy exchanged glances before standing up. They made their excuses and left the cabin.

CHAPTER 14

"Miserable Mary and her friend are going to be great craic on this trip, I don't think," Cathy said, as they walked away.

"I wonder why Mary is really leaving Ireland? Maybe her heart is broken, and it is making her appear mean?"

Cathy snorted. "That's your trouble, Kate Maloney. You always see the good in people. Like you never saw that the only reason Blake talked to you was to get you to lay with him."

"Cathy!" Kate looked around for fear someone had heard her friend.

"Well, it's true. I told you he had an ulterior motive for being friendly."

Kate didn't reply. Cathy was right as usual, but that didn't mean it hadn't hurt. She had believed the landlord's son was her friend and all the time he was just looking for someone to keep his bed warm until he found

69

a suitable wife. She wished him the best of luck but was still thankful Cathy had followed her that day. She didn't want to think of what could have happened, if Cathy hadn't come along when she did. She could still see the incredulous look on Blake's face, when she had refused to sleep with him.

She owed Cathy so much she thought, as she took her arm. They kept walking until they reached the central area Mr. Burke had mentioned. Kate came to a standstill, causing Cathy to walk into her.

"What? Oh, my word, Kate look how big it is. We'll have the most amazing parties. Look at all those seats, too. And it looks like we will have plenty of men to keep us dancing, too."

"Cathy!" Shocked, Kate tried to ignore the smiles on the faces of the men to whom Cathy referred. A few of them winked, while others smiled.

She dragged Cathy who was almost skipping with excitement over to the wooden benches and sat down. Cathy sat, but only for a second before she stood up again.

"Kate, there are all sorts on board, some French, German, and Italians, as well as those from Finland and Sweden. I've never met anyone from outside Galway until now."

"Cathy, will you be quiet. They can hear you."

"They can't understand me. I heard some of them speaking English, but I couldn't understand their accents."

"They still might know what you're saying."

Cathy rolled her eyes but took a seat beside Kate, and they were joined by some other Irish ladies, including their cabin mate, Mary.

Mary complained as soon as she sat down. "That steward over there was quite rude to me just now."

Kate glanced toward the man she indicated, but he seemed nice to her. He was smiling, and his eyes were gentle. She couldn't imagine him being rude, but, in the short time she had known Mary, she could imagine their cabin mate trying the patience of a saint.

"What did he say?" Cathy asked.

Mary sniffed. "He called us immigrants."

Kate tried not to look at Cathy, sure, if she did, she would burst into a giggling fit.

Cathy's dismissive reply to Mary didn't help. "It's true. We are."

"We are hardly the same as that lot." Mary puffed out her chest and threw a dirty look in the direction of the French and Italian travelers, Kate had been wondering about seconds before.

Kate wanted to say something clever, but she didn't get a chance. Mary was talking again.

"Eileen, it seems we are traveling with some bigwigs. John Astor, the millionaire, is aboard. They reckon he is the richest man in the world."

Kate didn't yet know how Mary and Eileen knew each other. They weren't from the same part of the country, with Eileen from Cork and Mary hailing from Dublin. Yet Eileen seemed content to let Mary do the talking.

"Yes, and he married a girl younger than his son. My friend worked at a big house in Dublin, and she said it was the talk of the drawing room. There were articles in the paper and everything. He divorced his first wife, the mother of his children, and then married this young one. They had to go to Europe to honeymoon. No decent family would receive them in America. Rumor has it, many of Astor's friends and colleagues snubbed him, when they did come into contact. Nobody acknowledges her as his wife, quite right, too. Didn't they know divorce is a sin?"

Kate turned away from the conversation. She didn't like gossip, and this particular lady seemed to have an opinion on everyone. Not only did Mr. Astor, whoever he was, not live up to Mary's ideas of a suitable traveling companion but neither did those who were sharing steerage. Mary continued to gossip, but now her subject of interest was the foreigners around them. Kate shifted in her seat, in the hope that their traveling companions didn't speak English.

"I'm looking forward to learning more about those sharing our quarters. America is full of people from all backgrounds. It will be good practice. Have a nice day, ladies."

Kate could feel Mary's eyes on her, as she walked away. She didn't regret speaking out. Learning about the Italians and other nationalities might take her mind off Nell and her beloved home.

ate watched as some of the men started playing instruments, from spoons to regular fiddles. Her feet tapped the floor.

"Cathy, look at that woman dancing. Do you know the dance?"

"Looks like a jig to me. Oh, I don't know that step. Maybe she'll teach us." Cathy stood up. "I'm going to join in. Coming, Kate?"

"No, thanks. I'll sit here and watch you make a fool of yourself."

Cathy stuck her tongue out, before throwing herself into the middle of the dancing.

Kate soon regretted her choice. The noise of the music and laughter didn't dissuade Mary from talking, her voice rising above the noise, Kate looked around for other people she recognized, but the lads must have gone exploring.

Disgusted with the conversation, she pleaded tiredness and made her excuses to go back to her cabin to take advantage of the relative quiet. As she walked, she met the same steward Mary had complained about earlier. Up close, he had a nice smile and kind eyes.

"Everything okay, miss?"

"Yes, thank you."

"My name's John Hart. It's my job to see you have a comfortable trip. So, if you need anything, just ask. Do you know your way around yet? If you are going up on deck, wrap up warm."

"I'm learning, but my friend has been showing me the way around. I'm tired and am off to bed. Tomorrow, I would like to go on deck for a walk, I think."

"Well, take this way, miss. That way leads to Second Class, and they have a gate. You can't get through."

Kate thanked him, and, having decided she was too wound up to go to bed, she took a walk out onto the deck. It was only slightly colder outside, but the fresh air was wonderful.

"Are you feeling all right?"

The priest's voice startled her. She'd believed she was alone.

"Oh, Father, I didn't see you there. You put the heart across me."

"My apologies for scaring you. My name is Father Byles. I fancied a bit of air. It's a great thing to see everyone having fun, but it can be a bit overwhelming."

Kate agreed. She stared at the sky, as the priest kept talking about the wonderful view and the lack of cloud cover.

"Have you been to America, Father?"

"Yes, child, more than once. It's a fine place. I take it, it's your first time traveling away from home?"

"Yes, Father."

"Are you traveling with friends?"

"Yes, Father, my friend Cathy, her brother Seamus, and a friend of his."

"Good. They will no doubt look after you, but, if you should need me, please call upon me."

"Thank you, Father Byles."

Kate watched, as the priest walked away. She didn't imagine needing the priest, but it was nice of him to offer. She turned her attention back to the sea and the sky. It was hard to distinguish where one ended and the other began.

Daniel walked toward her. "There you are. I thought you had gone to bed?"

"I was fed up listening to that woman. She was obviously behind the door, when they gave out instructions on how to be kind."

"You are even prettier when you are mad." Daniel moved closer. He reached out to push a strand of her hair behind her ear. She stood, her feet glued to the deck. She couldn't move.

"Kate, I know I should have said something before now but..."

Cathy appeared on deck. Kate wasn't sure whether she was relieved or upset, when she spotted Cathy walking toward them.

"There the two of you are. I thought I would have to

put up with Miserable Mary for the rest of the night. Thank goodness she found someone more important to speak to." Cathy didn't seem to realize she had intruded on anything. "Isn't this ship amazing?"

Daniel glanced at Kate, but there was nothing she could do. She couldn't very well tell Cathy to give them some privacy. She wasn't even sure what Daniel wanted to talk about.

Cathy yawned. "I'm that tired now, I could sleep on the deck. Daniel, Seamus has gone looking for you. He thought you had gone ahead to your cabin."

A flash of annoyance crossed Daniel's face, before he walked away without saying goodnight. Cathy didn't seem to notice.

"Come on, Kate, let's see if we can be asleep before Miserable Mary joins us in the cabin. I've got a feeling she might be going for a swim, if she keeps on moaning. I might just throw her overboard myself." Cathy laughed, but Kate wasn't really listening. She was still trying to guess what Daniel was trying to say before Cathy arrived.

CHAPTER 16

*K*ate woke early, astounded she had slept so well. Cathy was also awake, and the two of them headed to breakfast, where they found Seamus and Daniel.

Daniel looked up to acknowledge them. "Did you see the menu? We could be dining in one of those fancy restaurants they have in Dublin."

"What would you know of Dublin, sure you haven't been out of Galway until now?" Seamus teased back before shoving mouthfuls of Irish stew into his mouth.

Cathy made a face. "Stew for breakfast?"

Kate opted for the oatmeal to start and asked for some Swedish bread as well.

Cathy followed her example. "Might as well get used to foreign food."

Daniel stared at Kate. "What are you ladies planning on doing today?"

Something about the way he looked at her made her cheeks go hot.

"Kate hasn't any plans, but I'm going exploring. There has to be a way to see First Class."

Daniel shook his head. "You won't get through the locked gates."

Cathy simply smiled. Daniel shook his head.

"You can try using your feminine charms, but it won't work. The steward told me it's an American government requirement to keep the Third Class away from the First and Second Class passengers. It's their way to keep control over the spread of disease."

"Disease! They have a nerve." Cathy slammed her knife and fork down on the table. "I'm telling you, Daniel Donnelly, I will see First Class."

Kate intervened. "I'm sure you'll find a way, Cathy. In the meantime, why don't we go for a walk. I fancy some fresh air."

Daniel stood up. "We'll head to the deck at the stern of the ship. Cathy and Seamus walked ahead, but Kate stood still.

"Where?"

"Sorry, Kate. I meant the back of the boat. We have our own deck and the views of the sea are amazing. I wish I had some pencils to draw it." His cheeks turned pink, as he seemed to realize he had spoken aloud.

"You're an artist?"

"Not really. I mean I like to draw, but me da, he said it was a waste of time. Nobody makes any money from drawing."

Kate was about to mention a couple of famous artists, but the look in Daniel's eye stopped her. "What are you going to do in America?"

"I would love to work with horses. I'm good with them. Got plenty of practice at the big house, and the head groom, Foley, he told me I had a gift. The master, he bought this one racehorse, a magnificent animal he was. But nobody could ride him. He kept throwing anyone that tried. The master was beside himself, and he threatened to send him to the knacker's yard."

"No, he couldn't do that. Why would anyone destroy a healthy animal?"

Daniel's eyes turned to flint. "The rich have too much money and not enough sense. Anyway, I worked with Red, that was his nickname due to his temper, every day. Foley let me stay late. We didn't tell the master. He'd told Foley not to let a boy like me handle the horse. But Red and I had a connection. I'd love to own a horse like him one day," Daniel sighed. He stared out to sea for a few seconds before turning back to her. "You probably think I am an awful eejit."

"No, I don't. We all have dreams. Nell always said it didn't cost anything, so what's the harm?"

The expression on his face softened, as he looked into her eyes, "What are your plans, Kate?"

"Cathy said her sister, Bridie, knows someone who will give us a job in a sewing factory. Bridie's worked there for a long time and seems to do just fine. She has a place for us to stay, too, but in time I will have to find my own lodgings."

Kate didn't want to admit she was terrified. Cathy insisted Bridie wouldn't throw her out on the streets, but Kate remembered Cathy's older sister. She wasn't the nicest woman. Nell said she had a mean streak a mile wide.

"What is it? You look scared?" Daniel moved closer, taking her arm in his.

She was tempted to tell him she had read Bridie's letter. She hadn't meant to, but Cathy had left it lying on her bunk in the cabin. She wished she had never seen it. Then she wouldn't know Bridie had only offered to put Kate up for a week or so.

I don't have the time or money to house all the unwanted orphans from back home.

She closed her eyes, trying to clear that sentence from her mind.

"Kate, tell me, please. If there is anything I can do, you know I will."

She glanced toward Cathy and Seamus. She didn't want them to overhear her. Daniel must have realized she wouldn't speak in front of their friends, as he called over to them.

"Kate and I are taking a walk."

Cathy stood, as if she wanted to join them.

Daniel took Kate's arm, steering her toward the opposite side of the ship. "See you two, later."

At Daniel's comment, Cathy sat back down again, but her inquisitive gaze told Kate she would have to answer questions later.

CHAPTER 17

*D*aniel held onto her arm and steered her away from the others. He led her to a deserted bench and took a seat. She followed his lead. They sat in silence for a couple of seconds. Daniel turned to look at her.

"So, tell me why you look terrified?"

"Cathy's sister doesn't want me." Kate blurted out.

"Of course, she does. I heard Cathy telling you how Bridie was looking forward to making a fuss of you all when you get to New York. She sounded lonely to me."

Kate looked at her fingers, wondering what he would think of her if she admitted to reading someone else's letter. Maybe she didn't need to confess.

"That was all Cathy's doing. She has a heart of gold," Kate replied. "Bridie doesn't feel that way."

His fingers stroked her hand, as they spoke. She liked it.

"Kate, I know Bridie wasn't the kindest girl back in

the village, but that was years ago. America must have changed her. She is very generous to offer you a home and find you a job."

Kate grabbed her hand back, feeling ashamed. He took it again and clasped it in his.

"Take that look off your face, please. I wasn't blaming you or trying to make you feel bad. I'm not good at talking to pretty girls."

She smiled at him, though her eyes had filled up with tears.

"Kate, don't cry. I know you are scared, we all are. It's a new land and miles away from home, but it will be fine. Better than that. We will all make our fortunes, and in time we can go back to Galway, build a house, and raise our families." He stopped talking, his face crimson now. "I mean, if that's what you wanted to do, of course. You might prefer to stay in America."

She had to tell him.

"I read Cathy's letter. The one Bridie sent to her about the jobs. Oh, Daniel, she complained about having to find a job for me, and she said she wasn't providing lodging for me on top of everything else."

He looked shocked, his eyes widening as he answered, "She wouldn't do that. You're Cathy's best friend, and us Galwegians have to stick together."

"She did. In fact, her exact words were "I don't have the time or money to house all the unwanted orphans from back home.""

Rage filled his eyes, as he stared at her. She moved

back instinctively trying to put distance between them. He pulled her closer.

"I don't know why anyone would write something so horrible, but you don't need her. Kate, I have feelings for you. I have had them for a long time. I know you don't feel the same as I do, but in time you might. I swear to our Lord I will look after you in America. You will never be alone. I promise."

Kate couldn't say anything. Daniel moved closer, not letting her hand go. "We've known each other our entire lives. We can make this work. Marry me when we get to New York and come with me to Wyoming. My family will help us. My older brother Sean, or John as he calls himself now, has a large place. He sends mam money every couple of months. He paid for my ticket. America has been good to him. He will help me find a job with horses, and you can get work doing sewing or something until our family comes along. We will have a small place to start, some chickens and maybe a cow or two. What do you say, Kate?"

She couldn't say anything, it was so unexpected.

"Don't say anything. Just think about it. I have fifty dollars to my name. I don't know how long that will last in America, but you, I mean we, won't starve."

Although surprised at his outburst, she didn't feel offended. He was very nice to look at, and she liked listening to him talk. He had been tender and courteous to her, since they left Nell behind.

She listened, as he shared stories of his family with her.

Sean Donnelly had left Galway almost ten years ago, and she had limited memories of him. But he had seemed kind. All the Donnellys were. It was only Daniel who had teased her constantly at school and then whenever they met up. Nell said it was because he liked her, but he had never shown any signs of that until now. The picture he was painting of a tight-knit community was tempting, but could she marry someone she didn't love? She knew others did it all the time. The matchmakers back in Ireland didn't take love into account, when they drew up matches between families. It was more important to pick those who had small holdings near one another, so they could share resources.

She heard Nell's voice in her head as clear as day. *Love is a dream for those who don't want to go asleep hungry.* Nell hadn't even met her husband until the day she married him. Yet Nell was devastated when he died. Kate had heard how she mourned him. She didn't know about her own parents, her mother dying in childbirth soon after hearing of the death of her husband at the hands of the English.

She realized Daniel had stopped speaking and was staring at her, waiting for her to say something. She spotted Cathy coming toward them.

"There you are, Kate. I thought you had jumped overboard. I looked everywhere for you. What are you two up to? You look awfully serious?"

Kate couldn't help but be relieved at Cathy's voice. She smiled at her friend at the same time, as she let go of Daniels' hand. She smoothed down the skirts of her dress.

"We were just talking. What have you been up to, Cathy?"

"You will never guess. Turns out Seamus knows a guy who knows one of the stewards. He showed us the dining room in First Class. You should see it, Kate. It's a thousand times better than the one up in the big house. The tables are covered in snow-white linen. The silver cutlery sparkles in the sunlight. There is a big staircase, which leads up to a clock, with statues on either side of it. I wanted to go up there, but we didn't have time. I also wanted to see the deck, but the steward got scared someone would see us. There is a big, glass dome. It looks like a hotel or something out of a book."

Kate half listened, as Cathy went on about the sights she had seen. She knew her friend had big ideas about what she would achieve in America. She wanted a big house and a rich husband. What did Kate want?

CHAPTER 18

FRIDAY 12TH APRIL, THIRD CLASS DECK

"Look at that man over there, you see him?"

Delia looked in the direction Conor was pointing. She saw a tall man with a nice smile standing at the small gate which separated Third Class from Second. He was chatting to a lady on the other side of the gate.

"That's his wife. I was talking to him earlier today. He said he'd promised to bring her to America in style but couldn't afford to buy two, Second-Class tickets. So, he bought one for his wife and put himself in the cheapest cabin here in Third Class. He says it's so low down, it's a wonder they didn't give him an oar to help steer the ship."

Delia smiled at the joke, but she couldn't help wondering if the wife thought it was such a good arrangement.

"I wish I could have paid for you to go Second

Class," Conor said, pulling Delia closer to his side. Delia kissed his cheek.

"I'm glad you didn't. I wouldn't want to spend this journey with a gate between us."

The look he gave her sent thrills through her. Being married to Conor was wonderful, even better than she ever imagined. She missed him, when he went outside for a walk or a chat with the lads. She couldn't imagine not being able to sleep beside him every night. She loved being held in his arms, as they chatted about what they would do in America. She glanced at the lady in Second Class. She looked happy enough, as did her husband, but the thought of chatting over a locked gate had no place in Delia's marriage.

"What's the matter with him? He always stands over there with a look of misery on his face," Delia indicated the well-dressed young man who always appeared on the raised poop deck wearing gloves and a suit. She hadn't seen him exchange a single word with the other passengers, although she knew he spoke English. She had heard him speaking to a steward.

Conor looked serious, but his eyes were twinkling with merriment. "I think he's on the run. Maybe he stole the crown jewels and plans on making a new life in America."

Despite herself, she laughed. "Oh, you, stop teasing me."

* * *

LATER THAT EVENING they joined the merriment in the main lounge. She spotted a young girl with blonde hair dancing with a dark-haired, young man of a similar age. They were laughing and appeared to be very comfortable with each other. Once the dance had finished, they came and sat at the table Delia was sharing with Conor.

"Are you dancing?" the man asked Delia. She looked to Conor, who gestured her to go ahead.

"The name's Daniel, and my partner here, Kate, has a sore foot. She says I trod on it, but I swear it wasn't me."

Delia laughed, as Daniel joked around.

She didn't want to be rude by saying no. At the same time, she didn't want to upset Kate. "Do you mind?"

Kate blushed prettily, before shaking her head. "I need to catch my breath. Your feet are safe, but your lungs are in for a workout."

Delia soon knew Kate was right. The pace of the jig kept picking up, and soon Daniel was flying around the floor with her following his every step. He was a wonderful dancer, but she was glad when it was over. It felt odd for another man to be holding her. She thanked him, as he escorted her back to Conor.

"This is my husband, Conor Brennan, and my name is Delia."

"Daniel Donnelly, and this is my friend, Kate Maloney. We grew up in the same village just outside Ballinasloe in Galway. Are ye both from Dublin? You don't have the same accents."

Conor shook Daniel's hand. "The missus comes from

the posh bit. Nice to meet you. What part of America are you heading for?"

As the men chatted, Delia spoke to Kate.

"How is your cabin?"

"The cabin is lovely, but Cathy, our friend, keeps threatening to throw one of our cabin mates overboard. The woman won't stop talking about other people."

"Is it that awful woman over there, the one who could curdle milk by looking at it?" Delia put her hand to her mouth. She shouldn't have said something so nasty to this girl she'd just met, but Kate burst out laughing.

"Yes, that's her. Miserable Mary we nicknamed her. I swear she hasn't a good word to say about anyone or anything. Even finding fault with the ship and Captain Smith she is."

"For what? I think we are traveling in the height of luxury."

"I know, Delia. Can you imagine any other ship having accommodation as we have? Cathy, my friend, has been up to First Class. She said it was unbelievable."

"I can imagine, although the only members of First Class I've seen are the dogs being walked by the stewards. Seems they have to come to our deck area for their walkies."

The women laughed again. Kate's friend Cathy joined them.

"Seamus only asked Miserable Mary out to dance. Can you imagine it? I could have her as my new sister-in-law." Cathy rolled her eyes. Kate and Delia exchanged a look, before dissolving into more laughter.

All too soon the stewards announced it was ten o'clock. Captain Smith liked people to retire early. Delia arranged to meet Kate and Cathy the next morning for a walk. They wanted to teach her how to skip rope, something she hadn't done since she was a small girl, but they kept telling her she'd have lots of fun. It would give her something to do while Conor chatted with the men.

CHAPTER 19

SATURDAY, 13TH APRIL, DINING AREA STEERAGE

*K*ate couldn't find Cathy and the others. She walked into the dining area, hoping to find them. Instead she was greeted by the sight of a crying baby sitting on his mam's knee. His poor mother looked fit to cry, too. Kate moved to her side.

"Would you like a hand?"

"I would to be sure. My boys, little darlings that they are, aren't used to being confined. They prefer to be running around in the open air. Isn't that right, Frank?" The woman ruffled the hair of the youngest boy sitting on her lap. She then held out her hand to Kate. "Margaret Rice, recently from Spokane, Washington, but originally from Athlone."

"Kate from Galway. You live in America?"

Kate smiled at young Frank, as she spoke, but he stared back at her, his hand in his mouth. She guessed he was about two-years-old.

"We do indeed. My husband, God rest his soul, was

93

killed a while ago. He left me some money, and I used it to come back and show the children where I grew up. I have an uncle in Athlone. I thought it important the children got to see their roots. To be honest, I would have loved to stay at home, but there are more opportunities for a woman like me in Spokane. My husband left me a beautiful house and some savings back in the States. I couldn't be a burden to my family back in Ireland by giving them six extra mouths to feed." Her expression was so wistful, Kate had to hold back her tears.

Feeling sorry for the nice lady, Kate thought she could do with a break. She looked tired and no wonder with five young lads taking up every minute of her time. She spotted Daniel and motioned him over.

"This is Daniel, he comes from Galway, too. He's great with boys." She pretended not to see Daniel's eyebrows raise, so she kept her gaze focused on Mrs. Rice. "Perhaps the boys would like to play a game with us? We can take them out on deck, and you take a chance to have a cup of tea and a chat."

"That sounds wonderful. I think I have forgotten what a hot cup of tea tastes like. But are you sure? Five boys are a lot. Albert, my eldest is ten. He's is a good boy. He'll help you."

Kate pulled Daniel forward. "Albert, would you and your brothers like to go with Daniel, and I will take Frank? Your mam can have a rest."

Albert looked to his mam for consent, but the next younger brother hung back. Kate nudged Daniel with her elbow, motioning towards the child with her eyes.

Daniel bent down on a level with the child. "What's your name?"

"Eric, I'm six. Arthur is five, and he's George. He's eight. Can we see the captain?"

"We can do some exploring, but I am not sure whether Captain Smith is doing his rounds yet. Let's go check, shall we?"

The boys let their mother's skirts go and were gone without a backward glance. Kate took Frank into her arms, despite his protests.

"He wants to be walking all the time, but I worry someone will step on him in the crowd."

"I'll take him to a quiet part of the deck and let him run off a bit of steam. Maybe then he will sleep better for you. Albert, will you help me?"

The young boy nodded. Mrs. Rice gave her son a hug.

"Thank you, Kate. I am that tired, I think I would sleep standing up."

"You go and enjoy a rest, Mrs. Rice. Have a chat with some of the other women. We will be back later. Come on, Albert, let's see what Daniel is doing."

Kate enjoyed her time playing with the Rice boys. They were well behaved, especially given the constraints of the travel. A couple of the other lads on the deck joined in with the games.

Daniel threw Frank up into the air, making the child giggle. After a couple of turns, he handed the baby back to her. "That was kind of you, Kate."

"The poor woman to be traveling without her husband and all these children. She's a saint."

The look in Daniel's eyes made her flush. "You will make a wonderful mother someday."

"I best take you back to your mammy now, boys, or she will think I kidnapped ye." Kate spoke quickly in a bid to cover her embarrassment.

George pulled at Daniel's jacket. "Do we have to?"

"Kate, do you want to take the little one back in? From the look of him, he could do with a nap. The boys can stay here with Seamus and me."

Kate ignored Seamus's expression of distaste. "Thanks, Daniel."

Arthur stepped forward, shaking Kate's skirt with his hand. "Can I come with you? I want to see mammy."

KATE CARRIED Frank in one arm, and held Arthur's hand, as they went in search of Mrs. Rice. Spotting her at a table, Arthur ran to his mammy to tell her all about the games they'd played. Kate followed closely behind.

"I am so grateful to you, lass. I feel like a new woman. Were you good for Kate, Arthur?"

Arthur nodded but looked to Kate.

"They are lovely young boys. We enjoyed ourselves didn't we, Frank?" Kate tickled the youngster under the chin. Frank's eyes were closing, his thumb in his mouth once more. "I think this one could do with a nap."

Mrs. Rice took Frank in her arms. "Where are the rest of my boys?"

"They weren't ready to come down, so Daniel and the other lads are watching them. They'll be safe, I promise."

Kate sat with Mrs. Rice, as Frank fell asleep in his mother's arms. Arthur was almost asleep, too, clinging to his mother's side.

"It's hard for you to be traveling alone."

"It's my own fault, Kate. My niece, Catherine, was to come with me, but I didn't give her enough time to sort her papers. We had planned on traveling in May. The temptation to sail on this ship was too much. It's amazing, isn't it? I feel like I am in First Class."

"I've never been on a ship before, but we are certainly traveling in style."

"My husband would have loved this," Mrs. Rice's whispered.

"I am so sorry he died."

Mrs. Rice took a moment to compose herself, before offering Kate a wan smile.

"At least it was quick, an accident involving a train at work. The boys will miss him, to be sure. He was a wonderful husband and father. The priests say God has his own plan, but I find it hard to understand why he would take my boys' father. Still, there isn't time to be sitting around moping. It is what it is. Where are you and your young man heading for?"

Kate looked at the floor. "Daniel isn't my young man. He's a friend from home."

"Have you told him that? The way he looks at you, darling, I can hear wedding bells in the near future."

CHAPTER 20

$\mathcal{D}$elia made her way across the deck, having spotted Cathy and Kate. Cathy waved.

"Delia, over here. Join us for some tea and gossip."

Delia took a seat. "Afternoon, ladies,"

Kate rubbed her hand over Delia's sleeve. "You have beautiful clothes. They must have lovely shops in Dublin."

"Thank you, Kate. It was a wedding gift."

Cathy glanced at Delia, her eyes wide. "I think Delia is a bit above our station, Kate. She dresses like the ladies from the big house. Are you sure you shouldn't be in First Class?"

Delia clasped her hands, not knowing what to say. Kate came to her rescue.

"Cathy Madden, would you stop? You shouldn't be asking questions. Delia, just ignore her. Cathy, why don't you tell Delia about your plans to go on the stage?"

"I want to sing. I have a good voice, and I know how

to act. Just you wait and see. In a year or two I will be headlining in Broadway."

Delia smiled. "You certainly have the enthusiasm and personality. I think you will go far." She meant every word. She had yet to meet another person as infectious and full of the joys of living as Cathy Madden.

"And you Kate, what are your plans?" she asked. To her surprise, Kate looked terrified. Horrified she had upset the lovely girl, Delia opened her mouth to say something, but Cathy intervened.

"My sister, Bridie, is going to find us both work. I need to finance my singing lessons. Kate is going to find herself a husband and have children. She is a born mother. You can see that by the way she looked after those Rice children."

Kate blushed. "Cathy! Mrs. Rice needed a rest. It's not easy for her looking after five young boys on the ship."

Cathy didn't seem to see her friend was upset but turned back to the subject of Delia.

"So, how did you and your husband meet? I know you said you were both from Dublin, but you talk so differently. Are you sure you are not a rich girl in disguise?"

Delia didn't know what to say, so she decided on the truth. "I promise you I am not rich, but I did grow up in a house like the one you described working at."

Cathy, as expected, looked like she wanted to ask a million questions, but Kate just listened. Delia continued.

"I am an orphan. My parents were killed when I was twelve. I had to leave my home and go to live with my aunt. She is wealthy, and she expected me to act as she did."

Cathy's smile grew wider, her eyes glittering. "How wonderful. Imagine living with the toffs. But what made you want to travel in steerage. You could be enjoying First Class. It is so amazing. You should see the style they are traveling in."

"Cathy! Will you be quiet. You always say too much. Delia wasn't finished telling her story." Kate turned to face Delia, "I'm sorry. She gets carried away. It's none of our business."

"It's fine. My aunt decided I was to be married. She picked out my husband."

Cathy interrupted. "Was he rich?"

Kate rolled her eyes, as if giving up on her friend. Delia tried to frame her answer in an inoffensive way. Judging by the clothes Kate and Cathy wore, they would consider many people rich.

"He was what you would call comfortable, although he couldn't afford to travel up there in First Class. He was also a protestant minister and at least fifty years old."

"Fifty? He's old enough to be your father," Kate said.

Cathy's eyes almost bulged out of her head. "Protestant? But you are Catholic, aren't you?" For once, Cathy looked slightly unsure of herself.

Delia hastened to explain. "Yes, I am. A priest married Conor and me, but we had to elope. My aunt would never have allowed it to happen, and, being underage, I needed her permission."

"That's so romantic." Cathy gazed at her, a dreamy expression on her face.

"How did you meet Conor?" Kate asked.

"We grew up together. My mam ran away from her home and married a Catholic. She converted, and then they had me. We lived near Conor's family. I knew him from when I was a little girl. When I had to go to live at my aunt's home, he still came to visit me. He helped me with my chores."

"Didn't you have servants? I thought your aunt was rich."

Delia hesitated. "Yes, she was."

How could she explain what her aunt was like to these girls? "I mean she is. She hates me. I remind her of her sister and the fact she ran away. My grandfather had plans to present my mother at court and had arranged for her to marry a duke or something, but my mother ran away with my dad. My aunt never forgave her. She said it broke my grandfather's heart, and he died."

"Are you the granddaughter of an earl? And you gave it all up to travel to America in Third Class?" Cathy looked at her, as if Delia had lost her mind.

"Yes, and I would do it over and over again. I love Conor. He is a wonderful man, and we are going to be very happy together." Delia knew she sounded defensive, but she couldn't help it. Why did people judge others on the amount of money they had or whether they had a position in society?

Kate nudged Cathy. "I think it's really romantic, Delia. It's obvious you Conor and you belong together. You can see he adores you and vice-versa. Do you think you and your aunt will ever be reconciled?"

"No, Kate,there is no chance of that. She sent an armed man to Southampton to bring me home. Thankfully, she didn't guess we were traveling on the *Titanic* " Delia fell silent for a moment.

"You won't tell the others about this, will you? I don't want to be treated any differently."

"No, of course not, we won't breathe a word, will we Cathy?" Kate poked Cathy with her elbow, when the other girl failed to answer. "Cathy?"

"I'm not going to tell anyone, but how did you escape? It all sounds incredibly romantic. Kate's right."

Delia told them how her mother's friend, Lady Fitzgerald, had helped her.

Cathy gasped, her eyes wide. "I read about her in the papers. She was presented at court and was a real beauty and has two sons, doesn't she?"

Delia smiled at Cathy's knowledge of Irish society. "Yes, she does. She is still beautiful, inside and out. She bought me these clothes. My aunt used to make me dress in browns and other dreadful colors. Geraldine, I mean Lady Fitzgerald, was so nice to me."

"Why?" Kate asked.

"She was friends with my mother and said she did it for her. I think she would help anyone, if she could. Anyway, I wouldn't be here today, if she hadn't helped both of us."

Conor made them all jump when he asked, "Who wouldn't be here?"

Panicked, Delia tried to think of something to say. She didn't know if Conor would want her talking about their elopement.

"Your wife was just telling us about living in Dublin. New York will be so different from where we come from in Galway. We lived in a small town, didn't we, Kate?" Cathy smiled at Delia, as Kate nodded.

Delia relaxed, knowing the girls wouldn't betray her confidence. Still, she wasn't taking any chances. She stood up. "Thank you, ladies, for your lovely company. Conor, can we go for a walk?"

* * *

KATE SAT at the table in silence, thinking about the story Delia had told them. It seemed money didn't protect you from bad things happening.

"You're quiet. Are you feeling all right?" Cathy asked.

"I'm fine. I was just thinking about Delia. How sad her parents ran away together and then died so young."

"It is, but don't worry about it. We are young and about to start our wonderful lives in America. Nothing can stop us, Kate. We don't have any evil aunts hunting us down."

Kate couldn't share Cathy's enthusiasm. If only she hadn't read her friend's letter. Maybe then she could look forward to landing in New York.

CHAPTER 21

SUNDAY MORNING, 14TH APRIL, THIRD CLASS

*D*elia and Conor attended the Catholic mass. She waved at Kate, Cathy, and Daniel seated across the way from them. The English priest, Father Byles, and a German priest conducted the service. It was well attended, with every nationality in steerage being represented. Delia listened to the familiar Latin words, her mind swamped with memories of her parents taking her to mass when she was little, her First Communion when her mam had sewn an exquisite dress. She hadn't known at the time, but the material had come from one of the dresses from her mam's old life. She had felt like a little princess. She could still smell the incense and see her father's face glowing with pride.

Conor nudged her, when everyone else stood up. She was still kneeling, lost in her memories.

"You were miles away."

"I was thinking of my parents and how happy they would be for us to be together," Delia whispered.

Conor's expression changed, as sadness filled his eyes. "Not sure how they would feel about me taking their daughter away from Ireland, not to mention the fact we don't have a home or ..."

"Stop it right now, Conor Brennan. We will both get jobs and have a fantastic life in America."

"You're right, love. Someday, we could even be traveling up there."

Delia glanced to the First Class area. She had no desire to travel up there, but she would love to see it. Cathy's account of her visit to the First Class area was mesmerizing. She came back full of stories about a room where ladies could ride mechanical camels and a room where the staircase was as high as a building. Cathy had stolen a menu on her way back and a few passengers had drooled over its contents. Delia, although impressed at the variety of foods available, wasn't tempted, possibly as she had already tasted many of the courses at her aunt's house. She was happier than she had ever been, here in Third Class, with Conor as her husband.

The priest shook everyone's hand, as they left the service.

"Have a good day."

"Thank you for a lovely sermon, Father," Delia said.

He smiled. "My pleasure."

"Do you live in America, Father?" Conor asked.

"Oh no, I live in Essex, a lovely area of England. My brother is engaged to be married and asked me to marry him. My lovely parishioners raised the money for my fare. I am deeply grateful to them for doing so. As a priest, I wouldn't have the money to travel otherwise."

"That was nice of them, Father. They must think highly of you," Delia said.

"Are you traveling to family?"

"Yes, Father. Two of my brothers live in New York. They sent us the fare to come over. We were due to travel on the SS *Cymric* . It was canceled, so we were moved to this ship."

"Weren't we lucky? Not that I wish those men who are striking to be out of work, but sailing on the *Titanic* is such an experience. It will be something for you to tell your grandchildren. Now I must get going. It was nice speaking to you."

Conor and Delia watched, as he walked away. "He's a nice man, reminds me of Father Andreas. He has the same kind eyes," Delia said.

"Come on, Mrs. Brennan, I'm starving." He took her arm and headed in the direction of the dining salon.

"I think I am fitter than ever before, Delia. All that music and dancing is a good thing. I can eat as much as I like, and my brothers won't be calling me fat when we arrive."

Delia nudged her husband, "Nobody could call you fat, darling."

He made her laugh by pretending to preen in front of a glass window.

"How would your brothers feel about your jumping rope?"

He didn't rise to the bait. "You weren't such a good

skipper, I had to look after you."

"If my aunt could have seen me, she would have had a heart attack." Delia giggled. It took a couple of seconds to regain her voice. "At one point my skirts were up almost to my knees jumping rope."

"So I noticed." He leaned in and whispered in her ear. "I liked the view."

Delia jokingly pushed him away, but he just grinned at her.

"Your aunt sounds like she needs some fun in her life. Maybe she can travel out on the *Titanic* next voyage and see how to really live."

Delia hadn't said anything, certain her aunt wouldn't have traveled in Third Class. Even if Cecilia did find herself in Third Class, she would never have been caught dancing or skipping. She couldn't remember her aunt ever smiling. It's a wonder her mam had turned out so differently, when they both came from the same home. Conor put his hand under her chin, forcing her to look up at him. He smiled, but concern filled his eyes.

"Penny for them?"

"Not worth that much. I was thinking of my aunt and how she never smiles."

"Don't be thinking of that one. She's not right in the head. Thank God I got you away from her. To think you could be on your honeymoon with the reverend."

She nudged her husband, not wanting to think about that. She was so happy, maybe too happy. A chill crossed her heart, and she shivered. Conor looked at her, his eyes full of concern.

"What's wrong?"

She hesitated. Could she admit she was scared someone would steal their happiness. "Ah, nothing. I was just cold, that's all."

She snuggled closer to him and together they watched the antics of their fellow travelers, as the guy with the pipes weaved his way in and out of the skipping games, playing songs she didn't recognize but which seemed to be very sad.

Conor's stomach rumbled, making Delia giggle.

"I'm not being a good wife. I should feed you." She took his arm and led the way to the dining room. They found two, free seats near some other English speaking travelers.

Delia smiled, as Conor began eating almost before the server got a chance to put the meal on the table. She played with her own food.

"It's a beautiful day, isn't it? Do you fancy taking a walk around the ship, when you are finished?"

"Yes. You must eat first, Delia. We can't have you arriving in America looking half-starved. That would give my brothers something to talk about."

Delia ate to please her husband. She wasn't hungry and couldn't finish her portion. He didn't have the same problem.

"I best walk off that meal. Which direction do you want to take?" Conor bowed to her, making her giggle. She loved his sense of humor. She spotted Miserable Mary giving them a dirty look but just ignored her.

"I'm tired of being cooped up indoors, aren't you?"

Conor grinned, the expression in his eyes making her blush. "There are some advantages." He whistled, as they walked. When they came to the seating area, he pulled her onto his knee. She protested. "Conor, people are watching."

"So? We're married. Soon I will be so rich, nobody will care what I do. All they will talk about is my wife's jewels, her clothes, and how lucky she is."

She hated how he seemed to be besotted by giving her the life he thought she wanted. She planted a kiss on his cheek. "So long as we are together, I will always feel lucky."

She glanced up to find an older couple at the First-Class rail, obviously enjoying watching the steerage-class dancing.

Conor caught her looking. "We could sneak up there, if you feel like living dangerously."

"No, thank you. I have other plans for this afternoon." Glancing quickly around, she whispered in his ear. He drew back, his smile wide, as he brushed his lips across her forehead.

"Delia Brennan, I'm shocked. On a Sunday afternoon."

She knew he was teasing by the look in his eyes. Then he kissed her before saying, "Lead on, you wicked lady."

Feeling rather daring, she took him by the hand, and together they headed for their cabin.

CHAPTER 22

*D*uring a break from stoking, Davy poked Gerry in the ribs. "Have you heard the latest?"

Gerry shook his head, showering drops of water everywhere. He had just tried to cool his skin down, overheating as usual due to the fires.

"The captain's ordered full steam ahead. Despite the fact that the officers warned him there's ice out there."

"Of course, there's ice. It's the North Atlantic."

"Gerry, this isn't funny. I heard Barrett and some of the others talking. They're worried. The Marconi boys said some ice warnings came in earlier, but, rather than slowing down, the captain wants us to go faster."

"Captain Smith knows what he is doing. He's been traveling this ocean since before we were born." Gerry tried to sound more confident. He wasn't about to wind up Davy by agreeing with him. He mopped his face and head with a dirty rag. "Got any more of that tea? My throat is parched."

Davy handed over his cup, but he didn't say a word.

Feeling guilty, Gerry tried to reassure him. "Davy, stop worrying, will you? This is the *Titanic* remember. Soon we will be drinking cool beers in some bar in New York."

An officer chose that moment to walk behind Gerry. "You won't be drinking anything, son, unless you get back to work."

Gerry swore under his breath. That officer didn't drink alcohol and made his views of those who did well known.

"Sorry, sir." Gerry nodded and returned to work. He had to keep his head down and out of trouble Otherwise, Jeanie would have to kiss her ring goodbye. He needed a good report to get a job on the trip back.

He got back to his station and began fueling the boilers once more. Gerry glanced at Barrett. The man was staring at the pressure gauges. He'd never seen his chief look so worried. Gerry was about to ask why when Barrett caught him looking and gave him a reassuring smile.

Davy's worrying has my head turned upside down, Gerry thought, as he shoveled more coal into the furnace.

CHAPTER 23

SUNDAY EVENING, APRIL 14TH, THIRD CLASS

*L*ater that evening, Conor and Delia got up for dinner.

"It's awful chilly, isn't it? Much colder than last night," Delia commented, as she cuddled closer to Conor.

"Do you want to forgo our walk?"

Although tempted to go back inside to the warmth, she shook her head. Every evening after dinner they had walked the decks. She loved spending time with him, staring into the sky, wishing on the stars.

"It's such a clear night, the stars look so close, don't they?"

"They do, but that's not a star over there. It looks like another ship. Not a passenger liner, though."

"Is it? It looks tiny." Delia squinted in the direction Conor pointed.

He laughed loudly, causing her to look at him.

"My wife is thoroughly spoiled, having traveled

across the sea on the biggest ship ever built. Everything will look tiny to you from now on." He kissed her.

Delia giggled at his teasing. She was so lucky to have this wonderful man at her side. Conor gave her an impish smile before confessing.

"I didn't know it was a ship, either. I heard the crew talking."

"I thought you knew everything."

Conor winked. "I know enough to get by. Now come on, Mrs. Brennan, my feet have lost all feeling. Let's go below and show off our dancing skills?"

Delia grimaced, as she wriggled her toes. "After last night? I think I will be sitting it out. Kate, Daniel, and that crowd from Athlone and Galway could dance the legs off of you."

"They could, indeed, but they don't dance as fine as my missus."

"Oh you!" She took his arm, as he led the way back towards the sound of the party.

CHAPTER 24

*K*ate sat in the crowded, smoky, room watching the crowd dancing and having fun. She was in a funny mood and couldn't work out why.

A rat raced across the floor, as the women screamed and the men came running after it, trying to beat it to death. The women's screams turned to giggles, as the men turned it all into a game. Kate couldn't shake the feeling that everyone was just a bit too happy. She missed Nell badly, and the crowds around her seemed to increase rather than reduce her anxiety.. Daniel kept trying to get her alone, but she didn't know what to say to him. She liked him a lot, if she was honest, but was it enough to leave Cathy and move somewhere in America where she knew nobody. It would be different if they were still living in Galway. They would go courting for a while, get married, have children, and die without ever leaving Galway.

Here they were on the brink of a bright new future in an unknown land, and he wanted her to go somewhere she'd never heard of. But at least he wanted her. She still hadn't said anything to Cathy about her sister's letter. Cathy hadn't referred to it, and she didn't want to admit she had read her correspondence.

"You look like you have the weight of the world on your shoulders. What's wrong?" Cathy asked, as she returned from dancing to where Kate was sitting. Her friend took a large drink, causing Seamus to glower in her direction. Cathy retaliated by telling her brother to go dance with Miserable Mary. Seamus had declined, reminding her it was Sunday evening and nobody should be dancing and drinking on the Sabbath. Then he had left to go to bed.

Cathy retaliated by sticking her tongue out at his retreating back. "Maybe he should have become a priest after all."

Kate had seen Mary say something to Seamus early on in the evening, and, judging by the expression on his face, she assumed he had been hurt. She didn't enlighten Cathy, though, as it was none of her business. Then she spotted Daniel coming toward them. He had two drinks in his hands.

"Fine evening, isn't it, girls?" Daniel handed a drink to Kate. "I hear you've struck up a friendship with one of the Swedish men, Cathy."

"I wouldn't say that, Daniel Donnelly. We just had a few dances that's all. I didn't agree to marry him."

"Keep your hair on, Cathy. What's got into you?" He looked bemused by Cathy's reaction to his teasing.

"Sorry, Daniel. I had a fight with Seamus, and he got to me,"Cathy replied.

"Where is he?"

"He's gone to bed. I think I will follow his example." Kate rose, leaving the drink on the table.

"Why are you going?" Cathy asked.

"I'm frozen. It's much colder than it was earlier. I'm off to bed."

"Aw, Kate, you can't go to bed yet. 'Tis early yet, and we have hours more dancing ahead of us." Daniel tried to change her mind.

Someone came back in from the deck commenting, it was a beautiful cloudless night, the stars were shining and their reflection on the calm sea was mesmerizing. The woman suggested Kate should go and check for herself, but Kate declined. Too cold to think straight, she also declined Daniel's offer to walk her to her cabin. She needed to be alone for a while.

She made her way to her cabin, hoping she would warm up once she was under the covers. Thankfully, Eileen and Mary were fast asleep, so she didn't have to make conversation. She dressed quickly for bed and pulled the covers over her head. Soon she fell asleep.

CHAPTER 25

*D*elia's foot tapped away in time to the music. There were many different musicians from all nationalities traveling in Third Class. Although they couldn't understand each other's language, they communicated through music. The band was comprised of English, Irish, and Swedish musicians. One Irish guy had a fiddle and seemed to play faster and faster as the night progressed. The man took yet another swig of his drink.

"Must be the beer loosening up his fingers," Conor said

Delia didn't know how the man was still standing, never mind playing. He never seemed to be without his pint glass.

The atmosphere was so happy with different couples dancing jigs on the table tops. It had started a little like at home with men on one side of the room and women on the other, but, with drink flowing and the energy of the music, most were now up dancing.

Delia yawned for about the tenth time in a matter of seconds. Conor glanced at her.

"Are you ready to go to bed?"

She didn't want to spoil his fun. "I'll go, and you can stay here."

"Not on your life. Where you go, I go." He finished his drink "Lead on, lovely wife."

He gave her waist a quick pinch. She blushed, as she always did, when he touched her in public, but, secretly, she was thrilled she had this effect on him.

Daniel glanced up at them. "You're not leaving, are ye? Kate's gone to bed already, but surely the party is just starting."

"Thanks, Daniel, but the missus is tired. See you in the morning."

"*Codladh sámh*," Daniel said. "I guess I should head to bed soon, too."

Delia held her husband's arm. "They will make a lovely couple, won't they?"

"Who?"

"Daniel and Kate. They are made for one another."

Conor took her hand as the passageway narrowed. "I thought she was going to New York, and he was going somewhere else."

"That was the plan, when they got on the ship. They are from the same place in Galway. I don't think Kate saw Daniel as anything other than a friend until they got on this boat."

"Ship, darling!" Conor teased her gently. "I don't

think the captain would like you calling this vessel a boat."

They reached their cabin. "I can see the papers now. They will call it the *Titanic* romance."

Delia tapped him on the arm. "You aren't interested at all in what I am saying, are you?"

Conor closed the door, before he gathered her into his arms.

"I am very interested in you, my darling wife, but not so much in your friends. Kate and Daniel can sort themselves out. Now, I want to kiss my wife."

Delia gave herself willingly to his embrace.

CHAPTER 26

*T*he telegraph bell rang. Gerry glanced up. A red warning light flashed. *Stop!*

"Shut all dampers," Barrett shouted.

Almost immediately, the crew heard a horrendous crash. Gerry couldn't believe his eyes. Water poured from a gash, two feet above the stokehold plate on the starboard side.

"Get out of here, lads" Barrett yelled.

Gerry dove after the rest of his group, barely ahead of the closing watertight doors, as they slammed shut behind them.

Boiler room six was dry. George Cavell, a trimmer, greeted Gerry. "What on earth was that? Had to dig myself from under a mound of coal."

Another crewmate stared at an overturned bowl. "What a waste of good soup."

Gerry didn't reply. Soup was the last thing on his mind.

"Davy, you okay?"

"Yeah. What the heck happened?"

Gerry didn't know.

"Maybe the rudder fell off?" someone said. "We'll have to go back to Belfast to get that fixed. Should take a while. Nice bit of a break for us, eh, lads?"

Gerry shook his head in warning. Second Engineer Hesketh moved toward them. "All hands stand by your stations."

Gerry couldn't believe his ears. The man was ordering them back into boiler room five. Was he mad?

Barrett moved to Gerry's side "Gerry, after me."

Gerry followed Barrett and Second Engineer, Johnathan Shepherd up the escape ladder in number six. They would use it to climb into number five.

When they got to the top, they could go no further.

White faced, Barrett turned to Shepherd. "That's increased by almost six foot in less than ten minutes."

They got out of there quick, clambering back down the ladder into boiler room six. To Gerry's disbelief, the floor of the boiler room remained dry.

How could there be water in the next boiler room yet in here be dry? His eyes caught those of his chief, the expression on the senior man's face reflecting Gerry's own concerns.

"Shut the dampers, that's it, lads, shut the doors. Shut the dampers," Barrett shouted. Gerry worked just as hard as the others, praying intently as he did so.

"Draw the boilers," Barrett continued to shout. "Put

your backs into it. Gerry, take over. I need to check the coal bunker."

"Dear Lord, don't let them explode." The man to the right of Gerry crossed himself.

Gerry could barely see through the combination of sweat running into his eyes and the steam created by the heat, but he kept going. Who knew what these new boilers would do? They hadn't been prepared for an incident like this.

Barrett soon appeared. Gerry heard his report to Hesketh.

"Water's pouring into starboard side coal bunker, but pumps seem to be holding it at bay."

Hesketh nodded, his expression grave. He glanced toward Gerry, but he didn't meet his eyes.

The pressure in the ship's boilers started to rise. Barrett kept looking at the levels.

"The automatic safety valves will kick in. Any minute, now."

Gerry didn't know who Barrett was trying to convince, himself or the crew.

"There they go," Barrett shouted, as if anyone was in any doubt. The steam flooded the boiler room. Sweat flowed down Gerry's face and back. The excess steam flew up the steam escape pipes on the forward aft ends of the funnels. The noise was tremendous.

GERRY TRIED TO FEEL GRATEFUL. Maybe the men

around him were right in saying all would soon be back to normal, but something in his gut said otherwise. He tried to subdue those feelings and concentrated on the job in hand. Word spread that the men from the next shift were dragging their beds clear of waterlogged cabins. This made most people laugh but did nothing for the twist in Gerry's gut.

A few minutes later, leading fireman Barrett spoke. "I'm going to find Chief Bell. We'll have to inspect the damage. I'll be back. Keep at it, lads."

While Barrett was away, the speculation around Gerry intensified. The stoker working to his right mopped his brow.

"What do you think happened, Gerry? What did we hit?"

Gerry shrugged.

The man jerked his head toward boiler room five, "Was the water really eight-foot deep in there?"

That had been fifteen minutes previously. Gerry didn't want to think about how deep it could be now.

"Remember what Chief Bell said. Some compartments can flood. We'll still stay afloat." Gerry was surprised he sounded so confident when his stomach was churning. The water was rising. Would the bulkheads hold?

He picked up his shovel and kept working. Time ticked by and still no sign of Barrett. He glanced at the clock. It was almost five to one in the morning. He should be off shift by now.

Barrett arrived back, followed by Harvey and Shepherd.

"All stokers up on deck. Captain's orders."

The men stared at one another, before looking as one at Barrett.

"You heard me. The captain ordered the lifeboats swung out. Women and children only at this time. Off you go, lads."

The crew members left.

Gerry approached Barrett. He didn't want to be overheard questioning an order. "Are you going up top?"

Barrett shook his head. "I'll stay where we are. The engineers need help. They want to keep the lights going in the hopes another ship will find us."

A few stayed behind to help Harvey and Shepherd, the ship's engineers, with the pumps. Gerry was torn between going up top and staying with Barrett, who inspired him so much. He chose the latter.

Harvey ordered the men to lift up an iron manhole cover, so he could get inside to make some adjustments. More steam turned the boiler room into a Turkish bath, making the working figures look like ghosts. It was difficult to see. In his haste to check something, Shepherd fell into the manhole. His blood-curdling screams filled the air.

Harvey jumped to examine his colleague. "His leg's broken. Carry him over to the pump room, and let him rest."

Gerry and another man carried the injured Shepherd and placed him on the floor. They couldn't give him anything for the pain, but Gerry's friend gave him a tot of whiskey. They put a coat under Shepherd's head by way of a pillow.

"Thanks, lads," Shepherd's voice shook with pain.

Gerry's crewmate gave him more whiskey before taking a gulp himself. He offered Gerry some, but he declined.

"Don't say a word. The chief would throw me overboard,"

The injured man thanked them again, his pain evident on his white face. They didn't want to leave him, but Barrett and Harvey may need them.

"Now what do we do?" Gerry asked.

"Pray!" was the response from the man with the whiskey. They made their way back to where Barrett and Harvey were in deep discussion. Gerry kept his eyes on Barrett who was watching the instruments in front of him.

With a sudden roar, the sea came thundering through the compartment, the bulkhead collapsing. Harvey ordered the men to the escape ladder while he headed toward the pump room presumably in search of Shepherd. When Gerry looked back, Harvey had disappeared under the water. He took a step back down on the ladder, but Barrett pushed him forward. When they had climbed to the top, Barrett squeezed Gerry's shoulder.

"Lad, you've done your duty. I am proud to have served with you. Now go on, try to save yourself. It's every man for himself."

CHAPTER 27

*D*elia woke with a start. A strange noise had jolted her out of sleep. But what was it? A metallic scraping, not unlike someone tearing off the side of a tin can. Only louder. She strained her ears. There was no noise except Conor's gentle snoring. Had her imagination played tricks on her? Impossible to return to sleep, she slipped out of bed.

They had a two-bunk cabin, but, despite the cramped quarters, they preferred to share the same bunk. She made her way quietly to the door and opened it. The corridor was empty. Closing it again, she wondered what it was that was different. She looked out the porthole but couldn't see anything. Then she knew. She couldn't hear any noise. There was no vibration.

She sat on the bed. Conor woke.

"What?"

"The ship has stopped. At least the engines have gone silent." Delia picked at the cover on the bed, her stomach clenching, as she tried to fight her fears. "Conor, something must be wrong. A ship doesn't stop in the middle of the ocean."

Conor opened one eye. "What? You're imagining it. Come back to bed."

"Conor, I'm serious. Can we get dressed and check?"

Her words fell on deaf ears. He had fallen back to sleep. Her husband could sleep like the dead when he wanted to.

Grumbling to herself, Delia threw her coat on and went up on deck. The noise coming from the funnels was horrific. She saw a steward.

"What's happening?"

"Nothing to be alarmed about, miss. That's just the engineers letting off a bit of steam."

He moved away. She joined a group of women, but before she could ask anything, another steward came along.

"Back to your beds, all of you. Nothing to see here. You'll catch your death."

Delia was about to protest but changed her mind. The others were returning to their cabins. As she walked back down the passageway, she spotted a steward coming toward her, his face a mask of concern, until he saw her. He smiled as usual in greeting, as if it was an everyday occurrence to meet her in the corridor at night.

"What's happening?" she asked.

"Not sure, miss, but doubt it's anything to worry about. Why don't you go back to bed?"

Biting her cheek, she tried to stop herself from arguing with him. He must have sensed her doubt.

"Miss, go back to bed. You'll get me in trouble. Captain doesn't like people wandering about at will." The steward walked away. Delia watched him leave, before she opened her cabin.

Conor was still fast asleep, even the racket from the funnels couldn't wake her husband. Glancing at her watch, she saw it was a quarter after midnight.

She lay on the pillow and closed her eyes. Sleep eluded her.

"This is pointless. I won't sleep until the engines start again," she swung her feet out of the bed and squealed.

Conor shot up.

"What's the matter?"

"Water."

"What?"

"Conor, there's water on the floor."

"You must have spilled your drink. Go back to sleep, Delia."

She was about to argue when she heard a commotion outside. She opened the door to check. A woman shouted to her, "They've told us to get out. We've got to go up top."

Delia couldn't believe her ears. The empty corridor from a few minutes ago was now jammed with people.

She rushed to Conor's side and shook him.

"Conor, do you hear that? They are calling people to the lifeboats." She tried to control her tone, but her voice shook. "There's water on the floor. They are sending us up top. Get dressed in your warmest clothes, please." Her voice gave way. She pulled at him. "Conor, I'm scared."

"Delia, you have nothing to be afraid of. This is the unsinkable Titanic."

"But the water?"

"It's probably a burst pipe or something. Come on, back to bed with you."

He pulled her toward him. She pushed back. Anger and fear fought for dominance.

"Can you hear yourself? They called us to the lifeboats."

CHAPTER 28

*C*onor and Delia made their way to the Third-Class area, where hours before there had been lots of people singing and dancing. Some continued, but, in place of smiles, many looked worried. Some of the men said the water in their cabins had reached the height of the lower bunks.

She spotted a couple of foreigners arrive, all wearing lifebelts and carrying bundles. A man she didn't know walked over to the new arrivals.

"Would you look at the state of ye? Where do you think you're going?"

The men wearing lifebelts didn't speak English. They muttered and gesticulated, but nobody had any idea what they were trying to say.

"Delia, their clothes are wet," Conor said.

She stared closer. He was right. She caught herself looking at the women with children, seeing the fear on their faces made her stomach roil even more. She wanted to believe everything would be fine, but her aunt's curse kept playing through her mind.

"What's going on? Did someone ask the steward?" Conor asked.

"No stewards to be found." The stranger who answered just shrugged his shoulders and picked up his drink.

"I'll go up on deck to find out what's happening. You stay here where it's warm," Conor said.

She nearly fainted at the thought of him leaving her behind, even if he was trying to protect her.

"Not on your life. Where you go, I go, remember," Delia wasn't going to risk being separated from Conor.

They walked up toward the deck, but the gates were closed. A steward told them to return below. He insisted everything was fine.

"Why are they keeping us down here, if everything is all right?" Delia asked Conor.

"I don't know, darling, but it's bound to be nothing. This is the *Titanic* . She is the biggest ship afloat, unsinkable they call her."

Delia tried to believe him, but every instinct told her something was very wrong. She couldn't get the look on the first steward's face out of her mind. He hadn't known she was looking at him, and he had looked terrified.

"Have you seen Cathy and Kate?" she asked.

He shook his head, his gaze centered on their exit. She looked around her but couldn't see their friends. More people were coming into the lounge. Some of them appeared to be carrying everything they owned. There was a small group of people praying in one corner of the lounge, but, in the other, there was a group drinking and dancing, as if nothing out of the ordinary was happening.

Then the people started muttering, as another steward came forward. It was John Hart, the friendly man who had escorted them onto the ship. Was it only a few days ago?

"Ladies and Gentlemen, settle down, please. The captain has ordered women and children only to go upstairs. I will lead a group of you up to the boat deck before coming back for the next group. Please, ladies, come forward."

A surge of people moved forward, both men and women. The steward told the men to stay back, shouting at them when they didn't listen. Some other stewards arrived to help Hart.

Delia hung back, but Conor pushed her forward.

"You have to go, darling. I will find a way to get to you."

"I am not leaving without you, Conor," Delia held onto her husband's arm tightly. She couldn't bear the thought of going anywhere without him.

"Delia, don't be stubborn. Go with Hart, and I will follow behind. Go on now. Set an example to the other ladies. Please. For me?"

She hesitated.

"Delia, please," he begged. "I can swim, you can't."

"Swim?" she repeated, as all her fears threatened to overwhelm her.

"Darling we don't know what is going to happen, but

we have to be prepared. Now be a love, and do as you are told. Please."

She couldn't deny him anything. Giving him a hug and a kiss, she stepped forward. Some of the other women followed her lead, and together they followed the steward. She glanced behind her, when they got to the top of the stairs, but Conor waved her forward. He was smiling, but she could tell he was worried. She wanted to go back to him, but the surge of the crowd pushed her forward. When she looked back again, she couldn't see him.

ate didn't know what woke her. It wasn't a noise as much as a sensation. She sat up and listened. The engines weren't humming.

She glanced around the cabin. Cathy was sound asleep, as were the others. She turned over in bed, listening to the none too gentle snores of her cabin mates. Then she heard knocking on the door and a commotion outside. She jumped down from the bed and opened the door to find people streaming along the corridor.

"Get dressed and up on deck. They are loading the lifeboats."

She didn't wait to see who had shouted. She couldn't believe her ears. She turned back inside to wake Cathy, but her friend wouldn't get out of bed. She woke the other women, but they too told her to go back to sleep. She couldn't, though. She got some water and threw it in Cathy's face. That woke her. Cathy screamed her disapproval.

"Get up and dress. The people are going on deck. They said the lifeboats are leaving," Kate said, as she pulled her friend out of bed.

"What?" Cathy stood up, rubbing the sleep from her eyes. She looked at Kate, as if she thought she had lost her mind.

"Cathy, don't ask questions. Just get dressed. Come on. Hurry and put your lifejacket on." As Cathy hesitated, her voice grew firmer. "Cathy, for once in your life, do as you are told." Kate put her rosary beads and bag of clay into her coat pocket.

Cathy finally gave in and dressed, complaining the lifejacket was uncomfortable.

Holding hands, they made their way outside, leaving the other ladies behind. Kate gripped Cathy's arm, as the crowds deepened. She was terrified she would lose her in the mass of people. Then she spotted Seamus and Daniel.

Daniel pulled Kate toward him, giving her a reassuring peck on the cheek. "Thank God, we found ye. Come on. We got to get up top to the lifeboats. "

He headed back the way the girls had come, not releasing his grip on Kate.

"You can't get out that way, they won't let anyone through. They said we had to wait," a man said.

"Wait for what?" Daniel asked, but the man had moved on. Daniel pulled Kate along behind him. She clutched Cathy's arm. Daniel glanced down at them.

"I'm not waiting for anyone. We got to get out of

here. There's water on the floor near my cabin. Don't let go of my hand, you hear me?" Daniel ordered.

Kate nodded, she didn't look at her feet. She kept her eyes on Daniel's shoulders, following him through the mass of people. She didn't let Cathy's hand go either. Terrified, she tried to pray, as she walked, but she couldn't remember the words. How many times had she said the *Our Father*, yet tonight it was if she had never said it once?

*K*ate and her friends didn't get very far. There were too many people blocking their way. One Irishman ahead of them shouted "do or die," as he pushed forward against a locked gate separating Second and Third class. The steward guarding the gate looked terrified. As the crowd continued to surge forward, the steward ran off. The sheer volume of people moving, some screaming and some crying, was terrifying.

Kate's stomach clenched. "Daniel, I can't. There are too many people."

Daniel stood beside her, his gaze taking in everything that was happening.

"Kate, we have to find a way to the lifeboats."

"But they won't let us out of here. You heard the stewards. They said they would tell us when it was time," Kate hated how her voice shook with fear.

Daniel grasped her hand tighter. "It's time. I'm not

waiting any longer, and neither are you. Come on. Cathy and Seamus, you as well. Mr. Burke, are you with us?"

"Yes, lad, lead on, and we will follow. Come on, dear, I will take Sean, and you take the girls."

Mrs. Burke nodded, and the group set off following Daniel, who had taken control. They headed away from the locked gate. Everywhere she looked she saw faces white with fear. She clasped the bag of clay securely in her hand and began praying.

"Stop looking so worried." Daniel whispered. "We'll get out of this mess. Haven't we the luck of the Irish?"

She knew he was doing his best to keep her spirits up, but he couldn't hide the fear in his eyes.

"Daddy, I want to go back to bed, please, Daddy." Sean Burke's plaintive moan tore at Kate's heart. The poor child hadn't a clue. Kate clung tighter to Daniel. He made her feel safer.

"Shush now, Sean. We are going on a little trip on a smaller boat."

"But, Daddy, I like this boat. You said it was the biggest in the world."

Margaret Burke's clear voice rebuked the young boy. "Shush son, do what your daddy says."

"Yes, Mammy."

Kate exchanged a look with Mrs. Burke. Although Mrs. Burke sounded confident, the expression in her eyes told Kate the woman was terrified too. No matter how bad it was for Kate, it must be worse for parents with young children. What about Mrs. Rice? Surely, someone would help her with the children? She hesitated, she didn't even know where the Rice cabin was. Daniel pulled her along, so she had no option but to keep going.

CHAPTER 31

*T*hey all followed Daniel, and they made their way through a maze of passageways. All of them looked the same to Kate.

"How do you know where to go?" Kate asked.

"Don't tell anyone, but, after Cathy told us about her trip, I fancied a look at First Class myself. I got chatting to one of the stewards whose granny was from Galway. You should see it, Kate. All those women in their long dresses and sparkling like candles with their diamonds. And the food? I never saw anything like it. The carpets were so deep they almost came up to my knees. In the dining room, they...." He stopped talking, as they came to another gate, also locked.

A steward on the other side of the gate glared at them but didn't say a word.

"You shouldn't be here. Where do you think you're going?" another white-coated member of the crew shouted. Kate looked at his face. She thought he was as terrified as they were.

"To the boats. For the love of God, man, let the women and children through." Daniel begged the new officer.

Kate thought the man was going to turn them away, but, to her surprise, he opened the gates and motioned them forward.

"Take that way over there. Follow it the whole way, and you will come to a ladder. It's for the crew. Climb up there, and it will take you up to the boat deck. Hurry."

Seamus was inclined to linger, so Daniel chivvied him along. "Seamus, think of your sister. Come on now. Cathy won't go without you."

The Burkes were still following, only now Mr. Burke was carrying young Sean. Kate didn't realize she was crying until she tasted the salty tears. God, please look after us all, she prayed, as she followed Daniel, trying her best not to slow them down. Why couldn't women wear trousers rather than woolen skirts?

CHAPTER 32

*D*elia found herself at the head of her group, walking next to Hart.

Delia glanced at Hart but couldn't read any emotion. She voiced her fear. "It must be bad, if the captain ordered women and children to the boats."

"Board of Trade rules, Mrs. Brennan. If there is a hint of danger, lifebelts will be donned by passengers. The captain is being careful."

She half listened to him, as she tried her best to see if Conor was following them.

Hart escorted their group up the stairway to C Deck, across the open well deck, by the Second-Class library, before finally crossing into First Class. He marched through the C Deck foyer, before taking the grand staircase up to the boat deck. A woman in front of Delia stopped suddenly.

"Would you look at that?" The woman pointed to the

clock at the top of the staircase, flanked by two female figures."

"Imagine traveling in this? Wait 'til I tell Michael and the boys."

Delia couldn't stop herself. "Will you hurry up? When the crisis has passed, you can stand around admiring the view."

The woman huffed, but at least she moved. Delia caught a glimpse of John Hart's face, as he struggled to hide a smile.

"Don't think I would ever get a job as a stewardess, do you?"

"I don't know, ma'am. I think you would be quite good at giving orders."

On deck, there wasn't any real panic, but plenty of First-Class men dressed for dinner stood around in groups. She wondered where their women were. Some of the men smoked, but many just stared at something in the sea. When Delia followed their gaze, she was stunned to see lifeboats already out on the ocean.

A loud explosion made her scream. She looked to the sky to see something soaring high into the sky, leaving a trail of white smoke in its wake.

She glanced at Hart.

"Distress rockets. Captain must have seen a ship nearby and is sending for assistance. Come on. Let's get you all to the boats."

Hart kept going until he came to what he called boat eight. It was about to leave. Calling the crew, he handed over his charges to be put into the boats and turned to go back. Delia moved to the side determined not to leave the ship without Conor. She heard one lady speak to Hart.

"Are you not coming with us, Mr. Hart?"

"No, madam. There are more down below who need bringing up. I will be back shortly. Make sure you get yourself into the boat, now."

"Thank you, Mr. Hart. May God go with you." With that, the woman turned and waited to be put into the boat. Delia saw by his expression he must have been tempted to get into the boat, too, and save himself, but she guessed he had a duty to those he served. With a last look behind him, he headed back the way he had come. Delia kept looking at his retreating figure until he disappeared from view. What a brave man he was.

Nobody seemed to notice her standing beside the boat, and she watched with relief as the boat was lowered over the side. She wasn't leaving the ship, until Conor was beside her, holding her hand.

A crew member spotted her. He moved closer and whispered, "You should have gone in the boat, missus. There isn't much more time."

Delia pretended she didn't hear the man. Instead, she focused her thoughts on Conor. Should she try to go back downstairs to find him or wait for him here? The crowds milling about on deck made the choice for her. She wasn't going to risk getting lost trying to find her way back.

CHAPTER 33

Kate gasped, as the freezing air hit the back of her throat. She found it hard to climb the ladder up to the boat deck. Daniel helped her with every step. Her frozen fingers kept losing their grip. Several times he saved her from falling.

Kate scanned the view, trying not to panic. Her voice quivered, "Daniel, where are the women? There's only men on this deck."

Daniel didn't answer. He was looking over the rail. She moved closer to him. He wasn't far away, but the ground seemed to be slanting. She stared at her feet. Daniel put out his hand and pulled her.

"The deck is listing. Let me help you."

She looked over his shoulder. "Are there boats?"

"They've gone without us," someone cried.

Daniel took control. "There are more boats. Come on, Kate. You too, Cathy."

Kate glanced behind her. "But the Burkes?"

"They will follow. Kate, you have to get a boat."

She followed him down to the deck below. She spotted people ahead of her climbing out the windows. An officer, she heard someone call him Lightholler, stood with one foot in the boat, one on the A deck rail. There was a gap between the window and the boat. Looking down, she saw the sea. Shuddering, she tried to turn back but the press of bodies stopped her. Surely to God they didn't mean her to climb over to him.

"Stop. Get out," the officer shouted at a young boy.

Kate couldn't stop staring. He was only a child. Why would the officer not let him on. A man, dressed in a warm coat, protested.

"Of course, he is to go. He is but thirteen, and his mother needs him."

Officer Lightholler looked from the man to the boy and back again. He spoke gruffly. "He can go, but no more."

She didn't think she would be brave enough to set foot in one of the small boats. They were tiny, and the ocean was so big. Surely, they were safer where they were? She turned to Daniel to tell him her thoughts, but the look on his face scared her. Gone was the jovial boy she had become used to. A pale-faced version stood behind her. His gaze transfixed on the view from the window beside them.

"Come on, ladies, let's be having you. Get into the boats, now." The second officer ordered.

Someone grabbed her arm to pull her forward, but

she shook him lose. She turned to Daniel, wanting to feel his strength around her.

"I can't go, Daniel. I won't. I will take my chances. I want to stay here."

Daniel pushed her toward the boat. "No, Kate, you need to go."

"Come with me then." She didn't care if she sounded desperate. She was terrified. He looked at the boat wistfully, but then his expression cleared.

"I can't. They aren't letting the men in. I will get another one." He sounded confident, but he didn't look her in the eye. "You go now. Please."

She shivered, as they stood there. Seamus picked Cathy up in his arms and threw her into the boat. She was screaming his name, but he didn't take any notice.

Seamus turned to Kate and pulled her toward the boat, but then the Burkes arrived. Mrs. Burke screamed and kicked at the men commanding the boats. "My husband has to come, too. You got to let him go. He's a husband and father. My children need their father. Please, for God's sake, let him go. What sort of men are ye that you would make my children orphans?"

On and on and on Mrs. Burke screamed at the men, but nothing would change their minds. Daniel pulled Kate to him and kissed her soundly.

"You've got to get in the boat, my darling girl. Take this with you. He took off his Arran sweater and put it around her.

"No, Daniel, you'll freeze."

"I am made of hardy stuff, but you're only a bit of a girl. You're shaking like a leaf. Now go on with you."

She kissed him full on the lips and then turned away with tears in her eyes. A steward helped her into the boat, and then the order was given to lower away. Mrs. Burke had refused to leave her husband, and the girls and Sean wouldn't be moved. They clung to their parents.

She watched as Daniel went to throw one of the girls into the boat, but Seamus stopped him. He gestured to the father, as if to remind him that the child had both of his parents there to make the decision. The Catholic priests had formed a prayer circle. Instead of joining the boat, the Burkes knelt down and started praying. Daniel and Seamus joined them. Kate and Cathy clung together in the boat, as it was lowered away, horrified as they saw a number of people had also knelt on the deck praying.

"Jesus Mary and Joseph, look after my brother and Daniel and the rest of them. Please, God, keep them safe. I can't tell my mammy and daddy their son died on the ship. Oh, Kate, what will we do?"

ate couldn't reply. She pulled Cathy closer to her, and together they shivered and prayed with the others around them in the boat. A shout from the officer stopped the boat being lowered. The reason became obvious very quickly. Two women, who turned out to be sisters, were pushed into the boat, protesting loudly they wanted to stay with their younger brother.

"Our Mammy will never forgive us, if we leave the ship with him on it. You have to let him on or let us back onto the ship." One of the sisters protested, as the other tried to get back out of the boat.

"Shut up and sit down."

Stunned to be spoken to so rudely, the women sat down and started crying. Kate wanted to comfort them, but she couldn't think of what to say. The officer ordered the boat to be lowered. Kate prayed hard, although the sea was calm around them. She didn't feel safe in such a tiny boat. She wished she could have stayed on the *Titanic*.

She wondered if Cathy felt the same, but, before she got a chance to speak, a loud splash was heard off the side of the boat.

"Oh, Mary mother of god, Alice, that's Bernard in the water," one of the women said, as she rushed toward the side of the boat nearest the jumper. "He's our baby brother."

A crew member shouted at her. "Sit down or you will capsize us."

Kate watched the other crew member. He took up an oar. Thinking he was going to help the drowning man, she sighed with relief. Instead he started beating the swimmer about the head.

"Let him in," Kate shouted. The seaman paid her no notice. The sister who had spotted him stood up and made for the seaman. Kate watched incredulously, as the sister threw the man to the bottom of the boat and sat on him. She saw the woman hit the crew member with her hands.

She realized the other woman known as Alice was trying to haul the drowning man over the side. Leaving Cathy, she leaned over to help Alice.

A crew member helped them. "I'm in charge of this boat." The man used his oar to help drag the drowning man on board.

"What's your name," Kate asked the crew member.

"Quartermaster Perkis, miss. You best try to wake

him up. Sleeping after freezing in the water is a bad idea."

Kate looked at the saved man. He smiled before passing out, probably from the cold. Kate couldn't do anything more, so she returned to her seat beside Cathy. The two of them watched as the two sisters got the man sitting between them and rubbed briskly his hands and face until he woke up.

"Thank you." His weak voice was barely discernable. He closed his eyes again. Kate wondered if the man would survive. Someone handed the small family a blanket.

"Why couldn't that have been Seamus?" Cathy moaned to her side.

Kate didn't reply. She couldn't blame Cathy. Kate wished it had been Daniel who had thought to jump.

CHAPTER 35

*G*erry made his way up top. Everywhere there were swarms of people. Quite a few looked at him strangely, before he realized he had forgotten his jacket and was clad only in his vest and trousers, the uniform he wore tending the boilers.

A glance over the ship's side told him some lifeboats were already away. He couldn't remember his boat number. He could see a group of people climbing up the crane in the after-well deck, following others who were crawling along the boom to the First-Class quarters. He watched mesmerized. They looked like a line of ants.

A steward glanced at Gerry.

"Poor fools. It's the only way for them to get to the boat deck." The steward pointed to the emergency-crew ladder. "That's our best bet."

Gerry climbed the emergency-crew ladder, illuminated by the light coming from the First-Class restaurant, to get from the second deck to the boat one. He saw a young girl being helped to the next deck by a man in Second Class, allowing her to stand on his shoulders.

Gerry and the girl reached the boat deck more or less at the same time. He heard a sailor turn her away from a boat saying it was full. The girl glanced at the sea and then around her before she said, "My sister, she's in the boat. Please let me go with her."

"Sorry, miss, there is no room," First Officer, Murdoch, replied, "Lower away."

"Please, sir, I beg you. I have to look after her. I promised our mother. Please, sir."

Murdoch looked around him, before he gestured the girl to jump into the boat. "Be quick about it." He said gruffly. The girl picked up her skirts and jumped, landing in the middle of the boat.

Gerry looked down. The list to port was noticeable now. The gap between the lifeboat and the ship was about a yard and a half. A nearby crew member must have read his thoughts.

"That was some jump." The crew member manning the lifeboat station eyed the girl.

Gerry wondered if the story of the sister had been true. He turned away, but something made him turn back to face the officer. Murdoch looked around him.

"Any sailors?"

None appeared. Murdoch looked at Gerry.

"Can you row a boat?"

Gerry nodded despite never having held an oar in his hands.

"In you go then. Mind you get clear of the ship in

case of suction, but stay close, so you can come back if needed."

Gerry didn't answer but did as ordered and, taking a seat, thanked his lucky stars. His mam was obviously praying for his safety.

Gerry didn't look at the sea, which seemed to be many miles below them. His knuckles turned white gripping the sides of the little boat, wondering if he should have stayed on the ship.

"Lower aft," The sailors manning the ropes to the lifeboat shouted, followed by "Lower together" and then "Lower stern," Their skills kept the boat from tipping the occupants into the sea. Thankfully, they weren't crammed full and had room to sit down rather than stand. Then a shout from above and a body followed quickly by a second fell into the boat. A woman screamed in pain, when one of the men landed on her. Gerry didn't condemn the men, they had as much right to save themselves as he or anyone else had.

The seaman in charge of the lifeboat disagreed.

"Throw those two fellas out into the water."

Nobody paid the crew member any heed. The two men sat down, one taking the oar from Gerry and using it to maneuver them away from the stricken ship. Then they waited and waited.

CHAPTER 36

*H*earing the ragtime music across the water, Gerry stared at the stricken ship. Even though he had seen first-hand the water flowing in from the sea into the boiler rooms, Gerry found himself staring at the ship and almost believing there was nothing wrong with it.

"Maybe we would have been safer staying on it," a woman whispered to Gerry.

"No, ma'am. If you look there, you can see she is going down by her head." Even as Gerry pointed it out, they could see the water rising above the line of portholes.

The woman gasped. "You mean she will sink? But what of all those people?"

Gerry could see people gathered at the rail of the ship. Some were throwing things into the water, perhaps in the hope of using the items as rafts.

"Hopefully, a rescue ship will be here shortly,

ma'am. Captain Smith said there was one close by," a man answered. "That's why he sent up the flares, but the bug-" the man stopped just in time. "Excuse my language, ladies. They didn't answer. I know the wireless boys were trying to reach them, but they got another ship and they are coming as fast as they can. Can't remember its name."

The woman glanced at Gerry, but, although he could read the question in her eyes, he pretended not to understand. He'd seen the rising water in the boiler rooms but would the bulkheads hold? Maybe they would last long enough for the other ships to come to their rescue. He stared back at the ship, wondering how fate brought him here to this lifeboat, when so many were still on the ship.

The same woman handed Gerry a fur rap.

"Here, young man, take one of these. Not only are you not suitably dressed for company, but the weather is rather cold." Despite her formal tone, the glint in her eyes showed she was teasing.

"Thank you, ma'am, but, if you don't mind, I will give it to this young girl, she looks frozen already," Gerry didn't wait for the lady to agree. He wrapped the fur around the Third-Class passenger, a girl who was so thin, he could feel her bones. She didn't respond. Afraid she was dead already, he moved his hand closer to her mouth and nose. Relief flooded through him, as he felt her breathing. He wrapped the fur tighter around her, wishing he had some whiskey to give her to drink. That would help keep the cold out. He kept his arm around her, hoping they would keep each other warm.

CHAPTER 37

*C*onor waited impatiently down below with the other men. Tempted to rush the gates, he didn't want to suffer the same fate of the last man who tried. That man had been shoved back, fallen, and been trampled on by the crowd.

"Let us through," a man shouted.

Conor looked him in the eyes. "You heard the stewards. It's women and children only."

The man puffed his chest out. "My wife goes where I go."

The steward pushed in front of Conor and faced up to the man.

"Fella, I don't make the rules. The captain does. Get out of the way, and let those women come forward."

Conor got behind two of the women and shoved them forward. "Go on. Your men will follow. Go. Go!" He gestured with his hands, as the women didn't seem to understand English. The man, who wouldn't let his wife go alone, berated Conor.

"What are you doing saving them, bunch of immigrants with barely a word of English between them? No one will miss them."

Conor's temper flared. "Shut up."

"Make me." The man fisted his hands. His wife tried to hold him back, but he backhanded her. A red mist descended, and, before Conor knew what he was doing, he landed a punch on the man's jaw. To his surprise, the man fell backwards.

The steward half saluted Conor. "Couldn't have done better myself."

Conor turned away in disgust. He hated violence. He'd acted like his dad. The knowledge left a bitter taste in his mouth.

Sometime later, Conor saw Hart come back. His appearance meant Delia had to have got to a boat. Conor crossed himself. Now his wife was out of danger. He could concentrate on saving himself. Hart called out.

"Come on ladies. Let's be having you. Women and children come forward."

The other steward turned to Conor.

"We have to take the women and children. Captain's orders. Can you swim? There ain't enough boats for everyone. Don't tell anyone. Don't want panic down here."

Conor gaped at the steward. Had he heard right? There weren't enough boats. But that didn't matter. The *Titanic* was unsinkable after all, wasn't it?

166

The mutterings of the crowd got louder, as people protested against being kept below deck. Families pushed through with children, and old people were pushed aside. Chaos was descending, not helped by the fear and anxiety the sheer number of people was causing.

Conor helped to push some women forward to the stewards. Many women were reluctant to leave their husbands. Conor tried his best to convince these ladies.

"My wife is already off on a boat. Let your man go, and give him the peace of mind I have, knowing the woman I love is safe. If the time comes for us to make a swim for it, us lads will be better off alone than trying to fend for our women and children, too. Don't you agree?"

"But I can't leave him. He's all I got."

"Sure, he will be right after you, missus. You go on now, and he will be following behind in due course."

He was successful with some women, but others stubbornly refused to leave their men. Conor couldn't understand the men who pushed their own families behind them in their haste to get out. Once more, he found himself near to Mr. Hart.

"Thank you, Mr. Brennan. Your wife is on the boat deck. I saw to it myself."

"Thank you, Mr. Hart. I appreciate all you tried to do for us. May God look after you."

Hart shook his hand. "Best of luck to you, Mr. Brennan." Hart turned to retrace his steps to the upper decks, taking the group of women and children with him.

Conor sensed the men wouldn't wait much longer,

and he was right. The crowd surged behind him, and he was carried forward in the motion. The remaining stewards either fled or were forcibly knocked to the ground, as everyone fought to get out onto the deck, where they had some chance of being saved.

Conor knew he had to get away from the throng of people, or he could be pushed back into steerage or worse over the side rail of the ship. He clung to the wall and followed a slightly different path, behind some men who seemed to know where they were going. They arrived out on deck, but there didn't seem to be a way to reach the boat deck. The funnels acted as partitions between them and the boat deck. He then spotted a ladder. He started climbing only for the man behind to try to pull him off. He kicked out behind him and moved quickly to the top, where he found his way to the boat deck. He glanced at the water, seeing a number of boats already out on the sea. Were there any left? Which one was his wife in?

CHAPTER 38

Fear almost overcame Delia, as a group of men surged forward, trying to force their way onto a boat. The crew and officers were almost thrown into the sea in their attempts to push the crowd away from the boat. The crew was trying to fill the boat with women and children. At this rate, the boat would land in the water with nobody in it.

A shot rang out, followed quickly by another one and a third. The group fell silent in shock. Delia looked from the crowd to the officers, as one held his revolver up in the air.

"The next man who pushes into this boat will be shot. Do you hear me? Act like gentlemen, and let the women and children on, before we are all drowned."

Delia's heart beat faster, as she, along with the men and women around her, processed the officer's words. For the first time, someone had admitted the ship was going down. All pretense that this was just a safety exercise was gone.

Watching, Delia saw the realization hit the people around her. Some stayed standing near the boat, gazing at the officers. Some ran to find another boat. But nobody would test the officer's word.

The boat was quickly filled with women and children and then lowered away.

The officers and crew regrouped and moved up the deck. Delia prayed continuously for Conor to find her. She spotted Hart approaching the deck with another group of women and children. For a minute she thought he had missed the last boat, as the boat deck looked clear, but then she saw a boat about to be lowered from its davits. As Hart hurried his charges towards it, Delia searched the group frantically, trying to see Conor, but he wasn't there.

She saw Hart look behind him, as if weighing up whether there was time to go back for another group. She didn't think there was, and, even if there had been, where would he put them? Delia couldn't see any more boats. She watched, as Hart glanced at the officer in charge.

"Know how to handle an oar?" the officer asked.

Hart nodded.

"In you get. Watch out for the suction. Row out away from the ship and then stand ready for further instructions."

Without being told twice, Hart took his place in the

boat. Delia watched the boat being lowered away. She saw a couple of people jump and wondered if they had made it into the boat or had fallen into the water.

She didn't move, having decided here was as good a place as any for Conor to find her.

Just then Delia heard her name being shouted. Her heart leaped, as she saw her husband towering over the other men. She picked up her skirt and pushed toward him. Not only had she to avoid people, but at any moment she might lose her footing. The angle of the deck made walking difficult.

Rather than being overjoyed to see her, Conor looked furious. She threw herself into his arms. He stumbled but caught hold of her.

"Conor. I was looking for you everywhere. I couldn't leave. Please don't be angry with me. I love you."

The anger in his face was replaced by despair. He looked around him before turning his attention back to her.

"Delia, darling, you should have been in that boat. You can't stay here. You can't even swim."

"I didn't want to leave without you. I promised to be your wife in sickness and in health, in..."

"Yes, I know, I was there but, darling, you have to go. Come on," Conor half-dragged, half-carried her farther up the deck toward a boat.

He kissed her, holding her as close as possible. When he released her, he held her gaze. "You are going in this one."

She didn't get a chance to argue, as he said, "You promised to obey, remember?"

She nodded, but she didn't want to let him go. She didn't care about living, if he wasn't with her. He pushed her farther toward the boat surrounded by a ring of sailors who were guarding it against another mob attack.

"The officer threatened to shoot some men earlier, as the crowd got out of control. They became quite vicious due to fear of drowning."

"Nobody is going to shoot you, Delia. You are a woman and should be in the boat. Now, no more excuses."

Captain Smith stood to the left of her.

"Why are you still on the ship, madam?" The captain addressed a lady with a broken arm.

The lady, who was obviously a First-Class passenger, given her clothes, looked at the captain with disdain. "Some of us refuse to leave our husbands," she retorted.

Delia could understand the woman, but her reply angered Captain Smith even more. "How can your husband save himself and you, too, you with the broken arm. Get into the boat, and give your husband a chance to save himself later."

The woman, with tears in her eyes, clung to her husband for a long minute. With a sob, she tore herself away and moved to stand beside Delia.

Another couple stood to the side of the boat. The woman with the broken arm stopped to speak to them.

"Mrs. Straus, you must get into the lifeboat."

"I won't be parted from Isidor. Where he goes, I go.

You get in, my dear. You are young and have a long life ahead of you."

Delia thought the woman would refuse, but at that moment her husband picked her up and threw her toward a sailor who pushed her into the boat.

Captain Smith turned and caught Delia looking at them.

"You, too, miss, into the boat with you. Wait, lads, one more lady for you."

She turned to say goodbye to Conor. He kissed her gently on the top of her head and helped her into the boat. At the last second a man broke through the crowd holding two, young boys, the surge made Delia lose her hold on Conor, and he was pushed to the side. The stranger thrust the youngest child into Delia's arms. The second boy, he threw into the boat before disappearing back into the crowd. The children didn't get a chance to say goodbye.

A woman, Mrs. Brown, came forward, but there was no more room. Before the sailors could lower their boat, the woman sitting beside Delia stood up and got out insisting Mrs. Brown take her seat.

"Mrs. Brown, you have children at home. Take my seat," the young woman said.

"But, Edith, I couldn't possibly," Mrs. Brown replied.

"I insist. You go ahead. I will keep Colonel Gracie company." The woman called Edith didn't look back but walked into the middle of the crowd and disappeared. Mrs. Brown reluctantly took the vacated seat.

Delia would have gladly swapped with the woman,

too, but for the child sitting on her lap. Conor wouldn't have liked it, but at least they would have been together. She buried her head in the child's shoulder, not wanting to watch, as they were lowered down to the sea.

CHAPTER 39

"She's going."

Delia looked up, not believing her eyes. The *Titanic* was almost perpendicular, the lights were still on, and she could hear the strains of music, although she didn't recognize the song. Then the lights went out and came on for just a second, before going completely dark once more. The ship seemed to fight for a few seconds more before giving up and sliding to the bottom of the sea. There was complete silence for what seemed like hours but was, in fact, seconds, before the most awful sound filled the air. Delia held the baby tight against her and pulled the four-year-old closer. She sung to him softly trying to distract him from the screams and prayers of the thousand or more people dying in the water around them.

"Please, God, save Conor. I know it's selfish, but I can't live without him. Please, God, please. I will do anything you want. I just need you to save my husband," Delia concentrated on her prayers, trying to keep the horrible sounds out of her ears.

Despite the starry night of earlier, it was difficult to see anything around them. The women in the boat wanted to go back to rescue some of those drowning, but the sailors refused.

"They'll swamp us," one cried.

A woman dressed in a fur coat protested. "But it's our husbands and sons. Ladies, we need to pull together and go back for them. Are you with me?"

Delia didn't get a chance to respond. As the sailor threatened to throw the woman overboard, the lady sat back down. Delia couldn't meet her eyes, although she wanted to return, too. It could be Conor in the water.

The cold ate into her bones. She no longer shivered but grew completely numb. How long would they have to wait to be rescued? Someone said another ship was coming for them but from where?

Delia heard a voice from the distance telling them to yell, so they could be located. It was difficult to see in the darkness. Delia wasn't even sure if it was a real person or her imagination playing tricks on her. Still, she yelled with all her might, and some of the women in the boat with her joined in. Together they kept yelling, until they saw a green light. Fourth Officer Boxhall identified himself and took charge.

"We need to transfer some of you to this boat. Come on, now."

Delia couldn't move. The children clung to her, screaming. The officer tied their boat to his, and together the two little boats rowed across a sea, now as flat as a pond. Not a rescue ship in sight.

$\mathcal{K}$ate couldn't bear to look, as the once-magnificent ship died. Yet she couldn't look away either. Seamus, Daniel, and the Burkes could still be on board. Had Delia and her husband escaped? She turned back to look at the ship, the music played by the band filtering above the air. As she looked, she spotted Margaret Rice carrying Frank, with her other children gathered around her. Kate couldn't believe her eyes. Nobody had helped the family into the boats. She didn't want to look but couldn't tear her eyes away from the horrific scene. As the ship tilted, Margaret lost her grip on the children. One by one, they slid away from her disappearing into the ocean. Kate screamed. Then, Margaret lost her hold on Frank, and the two tumbled into the water. Kate jerked her head away, her whole body shaking. Clinging to Cathy, she sobbed her heart out. Why hadn't someone helped Mrs. Rice?

. . .

THE LIGHTS on the big ship went out one by one, as it slid to its watery grave. At the last moment, the ship seemed determined to fight for survival, breaking in two before disappearing beneath the ocean.

Silence reigned for a few seconds, and then the screams started. Kate had never heard anything like it in her life. She wanted to put her hands over her ears, but she knew she would still hear it. People were still alive in the water.

Quartermaster Perkis steered the lifeboat back toward where the ship had gone down. One by one, they pulled several swimmers over the side. In total, they rescued over ten men from the water, all crew judging by their clothes.

Kate helped where she could. The men were frozen, so she distributed the few blankets on board. The Quartermaster ordered his men to row away from the scene. "We got to get away now. Otherwise, we will be swamped."

Kate knew he was doing what he thought best. He had tried to help.

She took over the rowing from one of the crew who seemed to be going in circles. She couldn't be any worse. At least it would keep her warm. Then her hands grew sore, she could feel the blisters, so she gratefully gave up the oar to another volunteer.

Kate hugged Cathy tight, worried her friend was losing the will to survive. She urged Cathy to take a turn with the oars, but her friend refused, despite Kate telling her it would keep her warm.

There was nothing to eat or drink in the boat, and they were all dying of thirst. Someone wanted to drink the seawater, but the sailor warned them not to.

"That water will drive you mad. There's a big ship on its way to rescue us. It'll be here at any moment. Just you wait and see."

They didn't see anything other than ice floating on the surface of the ocean. A couple of people in the boat died. Kate could see the nice crewmen closing their eyes and saying a prayer over the bodies. Still, nobody spoke loudly. They all seemed to be conserving their energy.

As time went on, Kate saw a number of their party with bleeding, cracked lips. She glanced at Cathy, horrified to see blood running down her friend's chin. She wiped the blood away with the edge of her dress.

"Look, Cathy, look?" Kate pointed at the sky turning pink as dawn broke. "It's morning. Surely the rescue ship will come now."

Cathy didn't answer. She didn't cry or make any sound but stared at the bottom of the boat. Kate rubbed her hands briskly and put her arm around her, trying to combine their body heat. The girl never reacted.

"That's a ship," a man cried out. "It's come to save us."

"Do you hear that, Cathy? We are saved."

But Cathy didn't respond. Kate held onto Cathy's hand.

One of the sisters noticed Cathy's lack of reaction. "Maybe she will be better, when she feels a solid deck beneath her feet and gets a drop of the hard stuff for the shock."

Kate hoped the woman was right.

Another woman leaned in toward Cathy saying, "Could be the men are waiting on the ship for us?"

Cathy's eyes widened, and she looked toward the ship with new hope. Kate didn't have the heart to tell her not to get her hopes up too high, especially as the ship was flying her flag at half-mast.

CHAPTER 41

Conor watched Delia's lifeboat, until he was satisfied it had landed safely on the water. Then he knew he had to do something. A mob of people stood, balancing themselves on the listing deck. What were they to do, now the boats had gone?

He heard a couple of men talking about shots being fired to stop steerage men going in the boats.

"A young officer, name of Lowe, fired into the air. He didn't hit anyone, but the look on his face said he would if he had to."

"The officers had to get the women and children away. Would you want them to leave them behind?" A man asked, his tone suggesting the first man was a fool.

"Ismay was allowed on. He's a man ain't he? He owns this ship. He should have stayed on board and let fee paying passengers on the boats first."

Conor wasn't going to waste time listening to the men complaining. After the way he had seen the officers and crew man the boats and insisting on women and children only, he didn't believe for a second they had allowed the man onto a lifeboat for any reason other than he happened to be in the right place at the right time.

Some crew members were on the roof of the officers' quarters trying to launch two small collapsibles but weren't having much luck. "Do the best for the women and children. It won't be long now," a uniformed officer told his men.

A group of people knelt down in the center of the deck and started praying. Father Byles, assisted by other clergy members, gave general absolution. Conor knew the prayers by heart, but he couldn't just kneel down and wait to drown. He had to do something.

Stepping carefully to keep his balance, he tried to avoid the crowds surging toward the stern. His best chance of survival was not to be caught in the middle of a load of people.

Conor gripped the bulwark rail, unsure whether to cling on or dive into the water. A man came close beside him.

"Those boats don't look too far out. Reckon we could swim for it?"

"I was just wondering that. Should I jump or wait to swim off when she sinks?"

Crashing sounds came from inside the ship. They heard Captain Smith giving his last command to his crew.

"Men, you have done your full duty, you can do no more. It's every man for himself."

Conor and the man next to him exchanged a look. From somewhere deep inside the ship came more sounds, like that of muffled explosions.

"Reckon it's time to go. We could go under with the ship, and who knows if we'd be able to make it back to the surface again."

Conor didn't respond. He looked down at the sea and estimated it was a drop of about twelve feet. The lad climbed up onto the rail.

"Best of luck to you, mate." Then he jumped.

Taking a deep breath, Conor followed his example and dove into the water. Oh, divine Lord, but it was cold, colder than the Irish Sea even in December! It was a family tradition for his brothers and him and their cousins to go swimming first thing on Christmas morning. Conor concentrated on breathing and kicking, trying his best to ignore the cold. He had to get away from the crowds of drowning people in the water or they would pull him under. He kept going until he saw what looked like a raft. Reaching it, he discovered it was a capsized collapsible. He heaved himself on top of it. Only when he was stable, he grasped a nearby swimmer's outstretched arm and heaved him on.

The man stuttered with the cold. "Thanks, mate, my legs were so frozen, I didn't think I could move."

Conor glimpsed another guy and hauled him on as well. The three of them helped almost twenty more people onto the collapsible.

A man pointed to the ship. "Would you look at that?"

Their attention focused on the *Titanic,* as it slipped

fully beneath the surface. Silence prevailed for a couple of seconds, before the screams of the drowning people started again.

Conor wanted to help everyone but that wasn't possible nor practical. Every time someone came aboard the collapsible, it sunk lower into the sea until finally there was simply no more room for anyone else. Conor urged people to hold on to the sides, gripping one such swimmer himself. His arms ached, but he refused to let the older man go despite the man telling Conor to save himself. As the cold night wore on, those swimming around the raft lessened in number. Finally, there was silence around them. A couple of those rescued died, and their bodies were returned to the sea, thus allowing those who were hanging on by their fingertips to come aboard.

Later one of those rescued on the raft would swear Captain Smith himself swam up to them, a babe in his arms. He handed the baby to a woman on the raft, wished them luck, and swam away. Conor didn't know if the story was true or not, as he had not seen anyone.

*a*s their lifeboat rowed closer to the *RMS Carpathia*, they found themselves surrounded by up to twenty icebergs.

The woman beside Kate stared at the ice. "Look pretty, don't they? Who'd have thought they could be so deadly?"

Kate was saved from replying. The sailor heard the lady and answered.

"The small ones, they call them growlers. They be only ten- to twelve-feet long and about the same in width. The icebergs are between one-hundred and fifty and two-hundred feet. I think the *Titanic* must have hit a bigger one, miss." The sailor took a deep breath and whistled. "Captain of the *Carpathia* did well sailing around this lot."

Kate saw the passengers gathered along the rail of the ship, all staring at the survivors. The women appeared to be holding blankets and what Kate hoped was hot tea.

Even coffee would be good now, anything to take the chill from her body.

One by one, the occupants of her small boat were hauled up the side. Kate held Cathy's hand, while the crewman secured the rope around the girl's waist, and she was dragged up onto the *Carpathia* barely conscious. When it was her turn, she found the energy to climb up a rope ladder, after securing the now soggy bag of clay and the rosary beads in her coat pocket.

At the top, a woman with a kind smile put a blanket around her shoulders, handed her a warm drink, and led her toward the area for the Third-Class passengers.

"We got to keep classes separate, miss. The law says so."

Kate glanced at the steward. He didn't meet her eyes.

"I know you all went through the same thing. We'll look after you, don't worry about that."

She was going to ask him how he knew who belonged to what class, but he moved on. A female passenger caught Kate's eye and smiled.

"They think they can tell by the clothes you're wearing. Although that's not always foolproof. One poor dear arrived in a fur coat. The minute she spoke, it was obvious she didn't belong in First Class. Someone gave her the coat to keep her warm."

The First Class women were directed toward the staterooms in the care of the senior-ranking officers. The Second-Class passengers were directed towards their quarters, and then Kate and those of her class.

She didn't feel resentful. That was the way of things.

She'd no energy left to fight about anything. The woman handed her a warm drink.

"Sadie McKenna is my name. Are you traveling alone?"

She stared at her, taking in her silver-colored hair and kind eyes now looking at her with concern. Was she a survivor, too? She couldn't remember seeing her on the *Titanic*.

"No. My friend, Cathy, she was carried off the lifeboat just before me. She's in a bad way. We had to leave her brother behind and our friends." Kate choked. "One had five children with her. All those boys and nobody helped her." Kate couldn't stop the tears coming, picturing Mrs. Rice in her mind.

"Oh, you poor, dear girl! What sights you have seen! Come with me now, and we will get you some, dry clothes. Then you can find your friend."

"Mrs. McKenna, are there many survivors? Maybe our friends got off in another boat?"

The woman glanced from Kate to where the crew was pulling the now empty lifeboat on board.

"There are some. Most of the First-Class ladies and their children are accounted for, I believe. But the likes of us, nobody knows yet. All we can do is pray."

Kate couldn't pray. She didn't know how to talk to a God that let this happen. She changed into the clothes provided and carefully put Daniel's sweater to dry. If his brothers met the ship in New York, she would give it to them. If not, she would post it home to his mother. It was the least she could do.

"What will you do, lass?" Mrs. McKenna asked her. Confused, Kate didn't answer.

"I mean, will you go back to Ireland?"

"Never. Once we dock in America, I will never travel on the sea again." Kate swore she wouldn't. Once dry and with the blanket wrapped around her shoulders, she went to check on Cathy. Her friend had fallen into a deep sleep and was being well looked after. She went up on deck to keep an eye on the other boats still arriving. Maybe a miracle would happen.

CHAPTER 43

*D*elia didn't know how many hours they'd been in the water. How much longer could they survive without food and water? Daylight broke, but it didn't bring their salvation. The waves got rougher. Each one that hit the lifeboat threatened to swamp it. Delia bailed the water, as an older woman held the children, wrapping the baby inside her coat. The boys were frozen, like the rest of them. Delia had indicated to the four-year-old to keep his feet out of the water if possible. She didn't want the child to lose his limbs due to frostbite.

A woman pointed to something in the distance. "That's a ship."

The sailor in charge of their boat didn't even look up. "It's a star."

"She's right. It is a ship. Shout louder, so maybe they will hear us." Delia's hopes rose. They rowed faster and faster but didn't seem to be making much progress. They were tired now, and the rough sea wasn't helping, neither was the two feet of water inside their lifeboat.

"Row, ladies, faster now. We have a chance to live. Come on, now." One of the women cheered them on. Delia pulled harder with all her might. The children needed help soon, or they wouldn't survive.

Finally, they made it to the *Carpathia's* side. Delia's shoulders and arms ached from rowing. She didn't care. All she could think about was Conor. Was he already on board this ship? She glanced at her watch. It was a quarter past seven, almost five hours since the *Titanic* had gone down.

In addition to rope ladders, they sent down chairs for those who couldn't climb up and a satchel type apparatus for the children. It took a few minutes to convince the boys to get into the bag. They were obviously terrified. Delia did her best to soothe them, and soon they were reunited on the deck of the ship.

The crew was wonderfully kind, handing out blankets and a choice of brandy or a hot drink. Delia opted for the later.

Delia's teeth chattered, as she wrapped her hands around the hot drink. "Have you many survivors on board?"

"Some ma'am. If you follow that steward, he will take you to the Third-Class area. The ship's doctor will be with you shortly. Your children can go with you."

Delia panicked. "But my husband? I need to find him."

"Move along, miss, please."

"They aren't my children. They don't speak English. A man thrust them into my arms, as the boat was leaving."

The crew member looked from her to the children and back, his eyes sparkling with unshed tears, as he said gruffly, "They seem attached to you, madam, so if you could just keep them with you for now. Once we have pulled all the boats on board, we will best be able to reunite folk."

How could he reunite the living with the dead? But she didn't argue with him.

Delia carried the baby, and, taking the young boy by the hand, she followed the crew member to the steerage area. There, she recognized other Third-Class passengers who had danced and sung their hearts out at parties over the last few nights. Now they looked like ghosts. She searched the faces but didn't see Conor. He would have been easy to spot, not least as the room was predominantly filled with women and a couple of children. She gestured for the older boy to sit down while she changed the younger boy into fresh clothes someone had kindly donated. They were far too big for him, but at least he would be warm and dry. Then she saw to the boy. Only when the two children were wrapped in blankets, did she ask about Conor.

"Have you any other Third-Class passengers on board? My husband, he was left behind."

"There are some injured, ma'am. The ship's doctor is seeing to them. Some are in a bad way. Can you give me a description?" the steward asked.

Delia swallowed. Could the men not identify themselves? Pushing that thought to one side, she gave the steward as detailed a description as possible. He promised to come back to her shortly.

"Steward, the children with me are not mine. They speak another language. Perhaps you would know what it is?"

"I only speak the King's English myself, ma'am, but I know someone who might help. I will bring him back with me, as soon as I see if we have your husband on board. Now, why don't you see to yourself and get some dry clothes? You will catch a chill, if you don't."

Delia stared down at her clothes, all that was left of her possessions. She thought fleetingly of the new wardrobe of clothes Mrs. Fitzgerald had bought her. They were now at the bottom of the sea.

"Here, miss, here are some clothes that might fit you. The captain, he asked the passengers of this ship to help us out."

Delia smiled at the pale young English girl who held out a skirt and a white blouse to her.

"Thank you," Delia replied.

"I heard you tell the steward you were waiting on news of your husband. I hope you find him."

"Thank you. Are you alone?" Delia asked.

The girl shook her head. "I was lucky. I was traveling with my friend, and both of us were allowed on the same boat. I can't imagine what you must be going through."

Delia couldn't speak. She wanted to, but it was as if her brain was frozen.

CHAPTER 44

*D*elia changed into the dry clothes and hung her wet garments on a rack. She left her hair loose about her shoulders. She draped a blanket around her shoulders, in an effort to get warm.

"Your boys look like little angels, so they do." A woman pointed to the boys, sleeping with hands entwined.

Delia didn't correct the woman's assumption. She couldn't find her voice. She bit her lip, determined not to cry. Were these boys now orphans?

It seemed to take forever for the steward to return.

"This is one of our waiting staff. He speaks Italian and French. He may be able to help your boys," the steward said.

The man woke the eldest boy and spoke some words Delia didn't understand. Then the boy spoke, and soon they were having a conversation. Delia and the other steward waited for the waiter to translate.

"His name is Michel, and this is his younger brother, Edmond. His father, Michel Navratil, handed Edmond to you. Their maman is waiting for them, but she is in France. He says he doesn't know anyone on the ship." The waiter glanced at the boy, before looking back at Delia, "He said to tell you, thank you."

"He's welcome," Delia bit her lip in an attempt not to cry. She couldn't imagine how scared the boys must be, surrounded by strangers having gone through what they did. The steward left, saying he would be back shortly. Delia spoke to the boys, and the waiter translated, as they waited for the steward. He came back, a beaming smile on his face.

"A lady by the name of Margaret Hays speaks fluent French. She is happy to take care of the children, if that is all right with you, ma'am."

"Yes, please. I would keep them, but I cannot understand them, and I need to find my husband." She addressed the steward, but he wouldn't meet her gaze. "Nobody of that description is on board?"

"No, ma'am."

"Were there many rescued from the water?"

"Some were pulled out of the water alive. The freezing water was a too much of a shock for anyone to last long. Most died shortly after being rescued."

Delia turned away, not wanting to break down in front of the kind man. He put his hand on her arm. "Captain says we haven't picked up all the lifeboats yet, ma'am. Don't give up hope just yet."

Delia tried her best, but it was difficult. Every

survivor spoke of hearing the sounds of people drowning. Staying in the room with the other survivors became too much for her. She left to wait on deck, her eyes peeled on the horizon, hoping against hope she would see Conor again.

As she stared at the icebergs around their ship, all she could think of was her aunt's constant promise that she would bring disaster on anyone she loved. It was in her genes. Had her aunt been right?

.

CHAPTER 45

*D*elia bumped into Kate, as she made her way on deck. The two women embraced and then shared some tears, as Kate told her about Daniel. Kate asked about Conor, but Delia could only shake her head. They both looked to the sea hoping it would provide answers, as they stood at the rail holding hands.

Delia spoke first. "I've seen Miserable Mary on deck but not the other lady who shared your cabin."

"Yes, I've seen Mary, too, but I couldn't face going near her. I haven't seen Eileen. She was going to get married, when she got back to America."

"Kate, maybe we just haven't spotted her yet. There are so many people on this ship. I did see Eugene Daly, that man who played the pipes when we got on at Queenstown."

"Yes. I've seen him, too. Not many others, though."

As they stood on deck watching the sea, Delia couldn't tell how much time passed by. An occasional wail or scream made them look at the passengers around them. Most were in a shocked state just staring in front of them. Some were crying, but most didn't show any emotion. The passengers and the crew from the *Carpathia* couldn't have been nicer.

Then she saw the same steward she had spoken to earlier making his way to her. He was smiling. Conor. Did he have good news? Her heart beat faster, as she waited for him to reach her. A couple of people stopped him to ask him something, and she wanted to tell them to leave him alone, but she couldn't find her voice. Kate grabbed her hand and held it, an excited look on her face.

A wide grin lit up the steward's face. "Ma'am, there you are. I've been looking for you everywhere. I think we got your husband."

Delia could only stare. The man stopped smiling. He glanced from Delia to Kate.

"Delia, will you listen to the man? He says your husband is here. Conor is here."

Delia opened her mouth at Kate's urging but found herself unable to speak. Conor. He was here? But how? Where?

Kate grasped Delia's hands. "Delia, it's what we prayed for. Go find out now."

The steward waited. Delia finally found her voice. "Show me. Oh, for the love of God, is it really him?"

The steward blinked rapidly. "I think so, ma'am. He uttered the name Delia before he passed out or so the doctor said. We must hurry. You have to prepare your-self. He's in bad shape."

Delia didn't listen to his caution. Conor was alive! He'd been saved. She wanted the steward to run to where her husband was, but they couldn't. She had to be content with walking.

They got to the room where the sick were being cared for. Delia stopped at the door to compose herself before taking a deep breath. Whatever was wrong with Conor, they would deal with it together. Then she saw him. It was Conor, for he was wearing the same clothes as the last time she'd seen him. His beautiful black hair was almost as white as the pallor of his skin.

"Conor. Oh, my darling!" Delia took his hand. "Wake up, Conor. Don't leave me, please."

The doctor reassured her. "Your husband is sleeping. I gave him something to help. He was thrashing about, having nightmares, I'd imagine. A sympathetic gentleman gave up his cabin, so we will move you both in there. It will give Mr. Brennan time to rest. Once we are in New York, arrangements will be made to transfer him to St. Vincent's hospital."

Delia mentally thanked God and her aunt. God for saving Conor and her aunt for her insistence on good manners. She couldn't fall apart and wail, no matter how much she wanted to

"Thank you, Doctor, everyone is being very compassionate."

CHAPTER 46

Thrilled that Delia had found her husband alive, Kate couldn't stop hope from creeping into her heart. Maybe Daniel was in another boat and would be found. Seamus, too.

She stared at the *Titanic's* lifeboats, now gathered together by the crew of the *Carpathia*. She heard the crew talking amongst themselves.

"Dreadful isn't it? Some of them were not even half-filled. What was the point of them going off half-filled?" a crew member asked.

Kate didn't respond, as she assumed he hadn't even seen her. She simply listened.

"Heard some of them First-Class ladies saying they were looking forward to getting to New York. Poor souls believe their husbands will be waiting on the pier." The man knotted the ropes holding the lifeboats tighter together.

"That's madness. Sure, everyone knows we are the only ship to pick up survivors," his mate responded.

"Yes, I know that, but those women won't be told. They have convinced themselves there was a faster ship. God help them when reality hits."

Kate turned away. She didn't want the crew members to see her crying. She didn't believe Daniel and Seamus were on another ship but could understand why the women needed to cling to hope. Nobody wanted to admit their loved ones were dead.

Despite not wanting to hear any more, she didn't leave but continued to listen.

"You know Ismay survived. Shocking that. They say he spoke to Captain Smith and Chief Bell to get them to go faster, faster when there were ice warnings. At least Captain Smith had the decency to go down with his ship. Ismay pushed his way onto the boats and left women and children behind. So, they say, anyway." The crew member spat on the deck to show his disapproval.

"Did you hear that one First-Class fella bribed a group of the crew to give him his own private lifeboat, for him, his wife, their maid, and a dog. There're children drowned out there on that sea, but they saved their dog. That's rich folk for you!"

Kate turned away. She didn't want to hear stories like that. They hadn't been there. It was easy to condemn the actions of others. She moved farther down the deck, so she could no longer hear them. In four days' time they would reach New York. Despite it being overcrowded and full of people like herself, grieving and shocked, she didn't really want to leave. Yes, she wanted to get off the water and onto dry land, but that would mean facing up to the fact she was totally alone now. Cathy's sister was unlikely to have changed her mind about wanting her, and Daniel... he was gone.

Would it be easy to find a boarding house for women? She should ask some of the American women on board. They should know. She would manage. Alone?

She pulled herself together and told herself, God saved you for a reason. She half smiled, as Nell's voice rang through her head, as loud as if the woman herself was standing beside her.

She stood straighter. Daniel had believed America would bring all sorts of golden opportunities. She was young and strong, and she had survived, when so many had lost their lives. She would be fine.

CHAPTER 47

Kate stared at the peaceful ocean. It looked so beautiful. Yet it was deadly. A man came to stand beside her, his gaze on the Titanic lifeboats.

"Can't believe those lifeboats are all that's left. Said she was unsinkable, they did."

She glanced at him but didn't recognize him. "Were you there?"

"Yes, miss. I'm a trimmer. I qualified as a fireman, but I could only get a job as a trimmer. So many wanted to work on the *Titanic*. With the coal strike in England, those of us who got a job considered ourselves lucky."

"I'm sorry. I don't understand. What did you do?"

"It was my job to fetch the coal for the boilers. Bad coal it was too, 'cause of the strike. Maybe that's why this happened."

Kate didn't think so but wasn't going to argue.

"You were lucky to escape. I heard some men

207

discussing how those who worked in the engines would have had the hardest time escaping the death ship."

The man took a step back and growled, "I didn't dress up as a woman, if that's what you mean."

Startled, Kate looked closer to see his eyes watering.

"I'm sorry. I didn't mean to imply anything. A friend of mine, her husband survived by jumping into the sea. He found an upturned collapsible. He's down below now fighting for his life. The doctor said he was almost frozen to death by the time he got near him." Kate knew she was talking too much, but she felt she had to explain herself. She hadn't thought ill of him at all.

The stranger had the grace to look ashamed.

"No, miss. I'm sure you didn't, but there are some nasty rumors flying about this ship. There's those that are looking at any man who survived as if he should fling himself back into the sea. Maybe we should."

Kate grabbed his arm. "Stop that this minute. You survived, didn't you? What right do you have to take your own life? Yours is worth the same as anyone else's." When people turned to look at them, she realized she was shouting. "Oh, I didn't mean to shout at you."

"That's quite all right, miss. I don't mind what you said. It's nice to hear. I did what I was ordered to do. Chief Bell came down and ordered us to report to our boat stations. I couldn't find mine. But the officer on deck, he told me to go into a boat. He said I could help with the rowing. I ain't rowed anywhere in my life, but I did my bit. I just wish I could have done more. I wanted to go back and pick up them that were screaming for help. There was plenty of room in our boat, could have fit another twenty people, maybe more. But Lowe, the fifth officer, he wouldn't move. He said we had to wait for it to thin out a bit. A few of us argued with him, but there were those who agreed he was right in staying back."

Kate gripped the rail tighter. "Thin out?"

"Aye, miss, that were his exact words."

"I don't understand. What did he mean? Was it the ice?"

CHAPTER 48

A look of heartbreak came over the young man's face. Kate held her breath, not wanting to hear what he said next, yet knowing she had to.

"No, miss, he meant when there were fewer people. He thought we might be swamped, and our boat capsized. Said it was best to save those on our lifeboat than to risk more lives. So, we just sat there and waited and listened to the sounds of all those dying. The passengers, the lads I worked with, the men I served and my ..." the man couldn't speak anymore.

The tears ran freely down her face. "Your friends," Impulsively, she grasped his hands. "You didn't do anything wrong. It wasn't your fault."

Embarrassed she let his hands drop. She didn't know if he believed her or not, but she meant every word. She turned her attention back to the sea to give him a chance to compose himself. When he spoke again, his voice was still shaky but firmer.

"My brother was on the ship. He was the clever one in our family. Went to school for ages he did. Our da was alive then, and he could afford to stay in school. He was training to be an engineer. He was ever so excited to be serving on the *Titanic*," the man said, staring at the sea.

Kate pushed the lump back down her throat and squeezed her fingers around the ship's rail.

Davy coughed. "They say they died like heroes. It was them that kept the lights on in the hope a ship would see us and come quicker. They knew they had to keep the wireless going. Not one of them has come on board, not yet anyway."

"I think every crew member who helped someone was a hero." Kate took a second to compose herself. "More people were saved because of your actions. The engineers couldn't have done all that without your help and that of your friends, could they? I mean, I don't know a lot about boats, but you men had to keep the fires going to power everything."

"Boilers, miss, but I guess you're right." Davy didn't seem convinced.

Kate decided to change the subject. "My friends haven't come on board, either. Do you think another ship may have picked them up?" Kate looked him in the eyes. For some reason, she knew he would tell her the truth.

"This was the only ship to come near us, miss. Have you checked the list? Someone said Mr. Lightholler and Mr. Boxhall were making up a list of those saved. They are the senior officers."

"No, I haven't. I should, but..." Kate didn't want to

see the list. Not seeing Daniel's and Seamus's names on it would make it final. At least now she could cling to some hope. The man's intake of breath made her look to the sea. Another ship, smaller in size, had arrived on scene.

"That's the *Californian*. They say she was the ship nearest us last night. Her captain decided it wasn't safe to travel through the night. Not given the reports of ice."

Kate looked at the ship. Did it hold more survivors? She stared at it waiting. The man moved away to speak to an officer of the *Carpathia*. Kate's hopes died. It was obvious nobody was being transferred from the ship.

The man came back. "The crew told me Captain Rostron will say some prayers here and then head back to New York and leave the *Californian* to search for more survivors."

"You mean like a mass?"

"No just prayers. Someone suggested singing, but that made some of the First-Class ladies cry even more."

Kate could understand why. She didn't think she would be able to listen to any music again, without remembering the sound of the band on the *Titanic*.

Despite her anger at God, Kate attended the prayer service and was glad she did. Although very sad, there was barely a dry eye on the ship. For some reason it made her feel a bit better. Cathy missed it. She was still sleeping.

"Let her rest before she has to deal with the reality of losing her brother," Mrs. McKenna said.

heir new cabin was quite small, but Delia didn't care. So long as Conor was with her, she would cope with anything. She glanced at the doctor. He looked drawn and haggard.

"Thank you, Doctor, for taking such good care of my husband."

"Mrs. Brennan, you should prepare yourself."

Delia's heart stilled. She clenched her hands, to stop herself putting them over her ears. She had to be strong and listen to the doctor.

"Your husband is very ill. The exposure to freezing temperatures has taken a toll."

Delia whimpered. "Oh, Conor." Aside from his white hair, he didn't appear to be injured, just sleeping.

The doctor put a comforting arm on her shoulder. "He's a strong, young man, a fighter. While there is life there is hope."

The doctor shut the cabin door behind him.

"Did you hear that, Conor? I can't live without you. I want the life you promised me. I want our children to grow up with a loving father. Fight, Conor, don't you dare leave me."

She lay on the bed beside him, warming his body with hers.

* * *

CONOR BRENNAN OPENED his eyes to speak, but he couldn't. He could hear his wife's voice and wanted to speak to her, but his brain wasn't working. The urge to sleep was overwhelming, and he didn't have the energy to fight it. Every bone in his body ached. He let the darkness swallow him up.

* * *

AFTER FOUR THAT AFTERNOON, the doctor came back to check on Conor. He took a while examining him. Delia couldn't breathe. Was it bad news?

"He was lucky. We just buried four men. They, like your husband, were pulled from the sea."

Delia stifled a sob, staring at Conor. The doctor's ears turned red, as he apologized.

"Forgive me, Mrs. Brennan. I didn't mean to speak so plainly. It's been a very long day. Your husband is fighting hard. Don't lose hope now." And then the doctor was gone.

CHAPTER 50

TUESDAY

Gerry found Davy and a number of his other friends on the *Carpathia*. He was pleased to see Fred Barrett.

"Morning, Gerry. Glad to see you made it."

"Thanks, sir. We got lucky."

Barrett nodded and, making his excuses, left the group. Gerry glanced at Davy.

"Have you seen Tommy?"

Davy shook his head.

"Has anyone?"

None of the group met his eyes. Gerry's heart sank. How would he tell Jean and her mam?

"There was only seven hundred or so saved. We're the lucky ones." Davy said. "My brother didn't survive."

Gerry kicked himself. He'd forgotten Davy's brother was on board. "I'm sorry, mate."

Davy sucked on his cigarette. Then he threw the butt

into the ocean. "Did you hear Lightholler went down with the ship but then managed to swim for it?"

"No. That's good news. He has a kid, a girl I think." Gerry wondered why Davy looked angry. Surely, he didn't begrudge the officer his survival. Davy lit another cigarette, his shaking hands making it difficult.

"He'd a better chance than the French-and Italian-restaurant staff who were locked into their quarters. They had no chance."

Gerry's chest ached. His mind raced, and it took a few seconds to protest. "Davy, that has to be a rumor. No one would do that."

Davy looked him straight in the eyes. "Wouldn't they?"

Gerry couldn't respond. From what he'd seen happen in the last twenty-four hours, what did he know about how people would react?

"Gerry, how are you going to manage without wages? I have me mam to think about."

Gerry shrugged. "I guess Jean and I will have to wait to get married. I had some money saved for the house. We can live on that if necessary. Tommy supported his mam, so I will have her to look after, too."

Gerry's stomach rumbled. "Want to go find something to eat? You smoke too much."

Davy took a drag of his cigarette and blew the smoke at Gerry. "You sound like me mother. You go on. I need to be alone."

Gerry didn't push him. He had to find the surviving

Titanic officers. They'd be able to tell him how soon he could get back to England.

The officers, Pittman, Lowe, Boxhall, and Lightholler were chatting together near the First-Class deck. They looked at Gerry, as if he had grown two heads, when he came up to speak to them.

Fifth-Officer Lowe addressed him. "We've spoken to most of the crew and taken notes. Your turn will come soon enough." Lowe turned his back.

Gerry struggled to keep a civil tone. "I have some questions of my own, sir." How dare these men treat him like something the cat dragged in, when they had just gone through a similar ordeal?

But no matter how he phrased the question, Gerry found them reluctant to answer. They seemed to want to make sure the men were going to follow the White Star official policy.

Second-Officer Lightholler, obviously had had enough of him.

"The entire crew will disembark together when the time comes. We will be put aboard the *George Starr*, a U.S. immigration service tender. They will take us to Pier Sixty where we will join our ship to go back to England. The White Star Line has arranged for cabins on the Red Star Line SS *Lapland* for our trip back home. Good afternoon, Walker."

Gerry had no choice but to walk away, otherwise he would cause a scene. Although tempted, he glanced to his right and saw all the grieving First-Class passengers, mainly women and children. He couldn't add to their stress.

He walked back to where he had left Davy. People's reactions to a scene ahead of him jolted him out of his thoughts. He spotted a few of the crew sporting lifejackets, drawing gasps of horror from the *Titanic* passengers.

Davy and Gerry stared at the spectacle. "What the heck are they doing?"

Davy rolled his eyes. "Seems some rich guy by the name of Lord Duff-Gordon wants a photograph of all those who were in the boat with him."

"But there's only twelve of them," Gerry spluttered. He couldn't help feeling the photograph was in extremely bad taste. The sight of lifejackets had upset a number of the passengers.

"That's all of them that were in the boat. It should have held forty. The rich guy promised each man a five-pound note."

Stunned, Gerry turned to Davy, "You mean he bribed them to save him?"

Davy shrugged his shoulders. "Someone said it was to buy new kit."

Gerry knew it didn't cost five pounds to buy a new uniform. He stared at the people taking the photograph. The crew members looked uncomfortable, but Lady McDuff-Gordon and her maid didn't seem to notice. He turned away in disgust and decided to take a walk farther along the deck.

CHAPTER 51

*D*elia swung from anger to fear for the next twenty-four hours. She refused to leave the cabin to rest, terrified Conor would die alone. Some of the other passengers brought her food, and Kate sat with Conor, while Delia needed a break.

Two men came to see if Conor had recovered, both were second class passengers.

"Your husband saved my life, missus. I was swimming on my back and bumped into his boat. He pulled me on board with his own hands." The man rubbed his coat sleeve across his eyes. "Because of him, I get to see my boy grow up. I don't know how to thank him."

"No thanks are needed. Conor has always been like that."

"Same for me, missus. I didn't think I had a chance, The water was that cold."

Delia let them talk, trying to keep her face expressionless. Shame engulfed her, as hearing their stories made her angry not proud. She listened as they told her, Conor had been a hero, pulling people from the ocean onto the half-submerged, collapsible he had found. She was proud of him and furious at the same time. It was in his nature to help others. She loved him for it, but it had nearly cost him his life.

"Kate, there you are," Delia greeted Kate, as she walked into the cabin which was now rather crowded. "Thank you, gentlemen for coming to visit. I will let Conor know."

The men exchanged glances but left. Kate looked after them, a curious expression on her face.

"Sorry Kate, you must think I am horrible, but I couldn't take any more. They are the men Conor saved. I wanted to scream at them. Conor is lying here, because he helped others."

Delia flung herself at Kate, who held her, as Delia allowed the tears to come.

"Delia, you have to get some sleep. You've been through an ordeal, too."

Delia pulled herself together. Using a hanky, she dabbed her nose. "I'm fine, just a bit emotional."

"You missed the service yesterday, Delia. The captain arranged for a man, not a priest, to say some prayers."

Delia barely listened, her eyes glued to Conor's face.

Kate whispered. "I envy you."

"Me? Why?"

"You know what happened to your man. I hope he

survives, but at least you will know. My..." Kate couldn't continue but burst into tears.

Immediately guilt overwhelmed Delia. She wasn't the only one suffering. She put her arms around her friend and let her cry on her shoulder.

"I'm sorry, Kate. I've been so selfish. I didn't ask you about Daniel and Seamus. Is there no hope?"

Kate shook her head. "When you found Conor, I let myself hope for an hour or so, but the crew confirmed all the lifeboats had been traced. There won't be any more survivors. Nobody could have lasted this long in that freezing water."

"I am so sorry, Kate." Delia knew she was repeating herself, but what could she say.

"Daniel loved me and asked me to marry him. I should have said yes. He could have died happy. I don't even know how he died or whether they will find his body." Tears ran down Kate's face. Delia drew her friend down to the seat beside Conor's bed.

"I don't know what to say to you, Kate, only that I'm sorry."

"Daniel saved my life. He gave me his sweater. I was so cold, and he insisted. That's probably what killed him. He couldn't have lasted long in the water."

"Kate, don't do that to yourself. A sweater wouldn't have made any difference. The water was too cold. Daniel helped save your life. That's all you should think about. He loved you, and you are alive. You have to live your life for the both of you. Where will you go when we dock?"

"In New York? I don't really know. I was supposed to live with Cathy and her older sister, but Bridie doesn't want me. She didn't want me before now, and she definitely won't want me now. If Cathy had been traveling with just Seamus, he could have had my seat in the lifeboat. He would have been saved."

Delia's heart went out to her friend. "No, Kate, that's not the way it worked, and you know that. It was women and children first. He died, because he was a man."

"Yeah, a poor one. Look at how many rich men lived!" Kate's fierce response shook Delia.

"Kate, you are grieving, and it's natural you are looking for someone to blame but the reality is this ship is full of women thinking just like you. From Mrs. Astor right down to myself. If Conor had been in a boat, he wouldn't be lying here now. If there hadn't been a huge iceberg, if there had been more lifeboats. It's all ifs, and, if we keep thinking like that, it will drive us batty."

CHAPTER 52

*D*elia prayed and prayed, wondering all the time if this was her punishment for running away with Conor. Her aunt had cursed them both. Was he paying for her sins?

Kate came into the cabin. "Delia, take a break and go for a walk on deck to get some fresh air. If you keep this up, you will be dead on your feet when Conor wakes up. Go on with you. I will get you, if he wakes up."

Delia gave the girl a grateful hug. She needed some fresh air. Being below deck all the time was stifling. She strolled, finding out just how exhausted she was. Every bone in her body ached, but it meant she was alive, didn't it? She was surprised to find the visibility was very poor, due to a fog surrounding the ship.

A sailor looked up, as she walked past. "We are coming close now, missus. Should be docking day after tomorrow, if everything goes according to plan."

Delia nodded in response. She gripped the handrail, straining to see something. Then she heard her name being called. A breathless Kate ran up to her.

"Delia, Conor's awake and asking for you."

"I'm coming," Delia made her way as fast as she could to the cabin. Her heart beat faster, as she pushed open the door. Conor's eyes were open, and, when he saw her, he smiled.

"Conor, you're awake. Oh, thank God! You're finally awake."

"Delia," Conor whispered. His voice shook. He tried to sit up.

"Shush, don't talk. Conserve your strength. The doctor said to call him when you woke up. I'll go get him."

"I'll go, Delia, you stay with your husband." Kate was gone before she could say anything.

Delia gripped Conor's hand.

"Kiss me," he whispered.

She kissed him, as the tears of joy ran down her face. "I love you, Conor Brennan. Here, let me help you sit up."

When the doctor arrived, the look on his face, when he saw Conor sitting up, was priceless. Conor didn't have much energy, but his color was brighter.

"You are a fighter, Mr. Brennan. I didn't think you would make it, but I am very glad to be proved wrong."

"Thank you, Doctor."

The doctor did some checks, in particular of Conor's fingers and toes.

"The moment we dock, I'm sending you to the hospital. The freezing water and exposure have taken its toll. I would prefer it if you were kept under observation for a few days. Your circulation needs to improve in order to prevent permanent damage."

"He'll do whatever you say, Doctor. Thank you so much."

The doctor nodded and left. Kate hadn't returned.

"Conor, we are so lucky," Delia said, as she lay beside him.

* * *

Conor struggled to speak.

"Shush, Conor, we can talk later. Rest now."

He couldn't rest. Every time he closed his eyes, he was back in the water.

"It was like being stabbed by a thousand knives. Never did I feel cold like it. The shock seemed to force the air out of my lungs, I had to fight against blacking out. All I could think of was keeping my promise to you. I wasn't going to let you arrive in America alone."

Tears ran down her face. He tried to wipe them away, but he couldn't lift his hand. He gripped her fingers. "I love you, Delia."

She kissed his face and then his hands. "Oh, Conor, I thought I'd lost you. I'll never leave you again."

"I don't plan on being in another shipwreck, do you?" He tried to joke, but it was too soon. Their eyes met, both glistening with unshed tears. He didn't have the strength

227

to keep talking. He closed his eyes, not releasing his hold on her hand.

CHAPTER 53

Thrilled her friends had survived, Kate couldn't help but hope the news would help Cathy, too.

Wrinkling her nose at the smell of sickness and closing her ears to the sound of retching, the patients obviously feeling the effects of the rough seas, she found her way to Cathy's bedside.

"Cathy, I have the best news. Conor survived the sinking. Delia is with him. He's very sick."

Cathy didn't even blink. Kate couldn't hold back the tears.

"Cathy, talk to me please."

A woman screamed. Kate jumped up and rushed to help. She saw a couple of women shrink back in terror. Their would-be attacker held a club in her hands. "I want to die, and you'll help me."

The older woman's feet were bandaged, rendering her immobile. The younger woman moved in front.

"Leave mam alone. She's been through enough. Go away."

"If you do not help me, you die," the mad woman shouted.

Kate looked around, but there were no men available. As Kate took a step closer, the club-wielding woman caught sight of her.

"You want to die, too?" she shouted.

"No, but I understand you feel you need to. I will help you."

The women looked at her in disbelief. "You will?"

"Yes, but you must leave these women be. They can't help you. If you are intent on committing suicide, you really ought to do so in a ladylike manner." Kate mimicked Delia's accent, as she spoke hoping it would convince the woman she was upper class.

The woman nodded. "You understand. Thank you."

"No lady would jump overboard without a male escort," Kate continued desperately, making things up on the spot.

"No, they wouldn't. Could you please help me find someone suitable?" The woman looked so sincere and calm. It was hard to imagine that just a minute ago she'd been threatening to kill an injured patient.

"Why, of course, I will. You must promise to leave these ladies alone. They are steerage. They don't understand the ways of our class."

The woman actually sneered in the direction of the poor mother and daughter who stared wide-eyed at Kate.

Kate used the chance to run to find a steward, telling

him what was going on. He ran and came back with the doctor. Both men approached the woman, telling her they would be glad to help.

"Thank you, miss, for helping us. You were very brave. I was sure she was going to kill my mam."

"The poor woman obviously lost her mind. One can only imagine what tragedy she has seen." The mother said, rubbing her leg. The doctor arrived back to examine her, leaving Kate a chance to escape.

Despite the now windy weather and the resulting rough seas, she headed for the deck. She needed to be away from the smell of sickness for a while. It was a pity she couldn't run away from her thoughts, that it was only a fine line separating Cathy from becoming like that crazy woman.

CHAPTER 54

*J*n the days that followed, Kate heard so many theories as to why the ship had sunk, she didn't know what to believe. None of the *Titanic's* remaining officers would speak to her. She was told they didn't want to discuss the incident, until they filed their reports with the White Star Line.

She helped Mrs. McKenna with the other passengers. Her new friend told her she should rest. She wanted to keep busy, since it distracted her. Every time she closed her eyes, she saw horrific images play out in her mind. Mrs. Mckenna liked to talk, and, through her, Kate learned there were eleven brides on board who'd been honeymooning on the *Titanic* and who became widows overnight. There was another woman who'd lost her husband and son and yet another woman who had barely survived, only to find out her two sons had been lost. Possibly the saddest story of all was that of the Allison family. Mrs. McKenna's eyes glistened. "The babe and his nurse were in boat number eleven, but I guess in all the confusion, the nurse didn't get to tell the mother she had her baby."

Kate's chest hurt. She was curious but afraid. "What happened?"

"It seems Mrs. Allison and her three-year-old daughter, Helen, were in a lifeboat, but they got out. Mrs. Allison refused to leave the ship without her baby and her husband. The poor family, all three of them dead." Mrs. McKenna crossed herself. "At least the baby is rich. He'll not land in a workhouse or orphanage."

That was true, but Kate couldn't help feeling sorry for the tiny baby who'd lost his family. She knew what it was like to grow up without parents, but she'd been lucky to have Nell. What was the poor woman thinking now? The news of the *Titanic* sinking must have hit the papers back in Ireland. Yet there was no way for her to tell Nell she was safe.

Cathy sat on a chair with a blanket around her knees. Mrs. McKenna glanced at her. "Young Cathy seems to be recovering?"

"She's getting a bit better."

If Mrs. McKenna had known Cathy at home in Galway, she wouldn't have said the girl was recovering. That Cathy had gone down with the *Titanic,* leaving a shell of her former self behind. Maybe her sister Bridie would be able to nurse Cathy back to full health, when she arrived in New York. Cathy hadn't said a word, since they boarded the *Carpathia.*

CHAPTER 55

"Morning, Mrs. Brennan. I would say it's a fine day out there, but I'd be lying. There is a thick fog. The captain hasn't left the bridge at all. Still, we will be docked soon. I bet you are looking forward to being on dry land again."

Delia smiled at the steward. But for his bravery in escorting the other women and her to the lifeboats, many more would've died. She was thrilled he'd survived. "Yes, Mr. Hart, I am. Will you stay in New York for long?"

"I don't know the answer to that yet, Mrs. Brennan. I believe Mr. Ismay is working on getting us back to England as soon as he can."

Curiosity got the better of her. "Is it true the White Star Line stopped paying you when the ship went down?" She was immediately sorry, as the man blushed, his eyes darting around her. "I apologize, Mr. Hart. I shouldn't be so nosy."

Mr. Hart pulled at his collar, glancing around, before he

whispered, "Between you and me, missus, that is the truth of it, but I don't think those that make the decisions would like me to be telling you. Shocking it is, when you think about it. I was lucky, but my mates, God rest their souls, they got families at home, families that depend on their wages. Especially now they are dead. I worry about those families."

Distraught to be the cause of more distress for this brave man, she hastened to reassure him. "Maybe, someone will do something?" An image of her aunt's face came to mind. Not everyone cared for those in need.

"I expect so, Mrs. Brennan. I best go see my other passengers. You take care of yourself and your husband. I am so glad you found each other. So many lost..." His words faded, as no doubt he remembered all his friends who'd been lost.

LATER, a well-dressed woman with a cut-class accent approached Delia. "Would you like to make a contribution for the crew?"

"What a wonderful idea. I couldn't believe their wages were stopped, when the ship went down. What are they expected to live on?"

The woman looked at her blankly, her gaze raking Delia from head to toe. Delia could tell what she was thinking. Why was a woman with a similar accent wearing clothes obviously belonging to a steerage passenger? Delia didn't say a word but stared back until the woman recovered her manners.

"Oh, no, there's been some misunderstanding. This isn't for the *Titanic* men but for Dear Captain Rostron and his crew. We have collected almost four hundred dollars, isn't that wonderful? I know it's vulgar to speak about money, but we were so hoping we would be able to give him a large payment. Even five dollars means a lot to some of the crew."

It was Delia's turn to stare at the woman in front of her. Could she hear herself? Five dollars was a lot to most people. She was on board a ship with goodness knows how many survivors left with nothing but the borrowed clothes on their backs. What would she know about the value of one dollar, never mind five?

Afraid she would cause upset, Delia excused herself and walked hurriedly away.

A few hours later, Mrs. McKenna came down to the cabin to keep Delia company.

"I thought you might fancy a chat, Mrs. Brennan. Or perhaps you want to take a walk. I can sit with your husband."

"That's very kind of you, Mrs. McKenna. Please call me Delia. I would rather stay with Conor but would value your company."

"How is he? Kate said there wasn't much change?"

"No, but he is fighting hard."

"A man you can be proud of. I've heard numerous people credit your husband with saving their lives." Mrs. McKenna sat back in the chair. "Have you heard the passengers collected a large sum of money? They awarded Captain Rostron five hundred dollars. I believe each crew member received a sum of money."

"I knew about the collection. A woman approached me, while I was walking on deck. Captain Rostron is a wonderful man and a real hero."

"But?"

"The *Titanic* crew who saved the passengers are heroes, too. The woman I spoke to didn't appear to think so."

"She may have thought that was their job."

Delia couldn't stop herself from protesting. "Nobody should have to lay down his life for another. What of their families? And those who survived but with horrific injuries, how will they support their families? Did you know the White Star Line has suspended all pay?" Delia couldn't continue. Tears of frustration and anger choked her.

"Cry dear. Let those tears flow. You don't have to be strong all the time."

"I'm sorry. I didn't mean to attack you."

"No offense taken. You are completely right. In an ideal world, the men from the *Titanic* would be compensated. We can but hope it will happen in time. For now, you need to give yourself time to heal."

Delia swallowed the lump. "I have to look after Conor."

"Let us help, Mrs. Brennan. You may not have suffered physical injuries, but you have been through an ordeal."

Delia made the mistake of looking directly at Mrs.

McKenna. Pity and understanding filled the woman's eyes. Delia couldn't stop the tears from falling.

"I can't close my eyes. Every time I try, I see..." Delia put her head in her hands and sobbed. Mrs. McKenna moved to her side and rubbed her back, as Delia shuddered.

A few minutes passed before Delia's sobs stilled. Mrs. McKenna handed her a hanky. "Some say a good cry is the best medicine. Why don't you take a walk, get some fresh air, and I will sit here with your husband?"

Delia couldn't thank the woman enough for her thoughtfulness.

CHAPTER 56

*D*elia hadn't been long on deck, when she found Kate.

"Delia, is Conor all right?"

"He's sleeping. A passenger, Mrs. McKenna, is sitting with him."

"She's so kind, isn't she? She's helped with Cathy as well." Kate stared back at the ocean. "Not that Cathy is improving."

"It will take time for all of us to get over what happened, Kate. Don't give up just yet."

Kate gave her a wan smile. "Have you spent much time chatting to other survivors?"

"Not really. I might say the wrong thing to some of the women."

Kate looked at her, curiously. "What makes you think that?"

"I don't know if I am being oversensitive, but some women seem to think no man should have survived. As if by living, they were somehow less than a gentleman." Delia didn't look at Kate, for fear she sounded stupid.

"I thought that, too. I heard a couple of women call a man a coward for getting into a boat. He said he was ordered to do so. Some officer, Lightholler was his name, needed extra crew. This man was a yachtsman, whatever that is."

"I can't understand their thinking. Who cares how someone survived? The fact they lived is important."

"I wish Daniel had thought to swim or jump into a boat. Seamus, too."

"Oh, Kate, forgive me for opening my big mouth. I didn't mean to remind you."

"I don't need reminding. I don't think I will ever forget."

Delia took Kate's hand in hers. Together they stared at the ocean for a while.

"I best get back to Conor. Talk to you later."

As SHE HEADED DOWN BELOW, Delia knew she wouldn't have cared how Conor survived, so long as he lived. She had nothing but pity for Mr. Ismay, despite the gossip on board the *Carpathia*. The man had helped lots of women and children into the boats. She had seen that for herself and heard it from others. If there were no more women and children around and yet a space in the boat, why should he have not saved himself?

. . .

AFTER FOUR DAYS on board and eight since they had left Queenstown, the *Titanic* survivors arrived in New York. Delia, with Conor standing by her side, leaning on her for support, watched as the sea in front of them was filled with tugboats of every size. They were filled with reporters and those taking photographs, their magnesium bombs flashing like a Morse lamp.

Worried her husband would be standing too long, Delia tried to get him to go below. "Mr. Hart said the captain had to put off the Titanic lifeboats first, at the White Star area. Then he will sail to the Cunard pier, where we will be escorted off. We will be ages yet. Please go below."

"And miss seeing America for the first time." He smiled. "Delia, I'm fine. I might be able to spot my brothers."

"Don't forget, the doctor said you have to go to the hospital."

"I know, love, but first we have to get through customs clearance."

"No, we don't. It's been suspended due to the unusual circumstances of our trip. I guess they are trying to spare us."

Conor looked up to heaven but didn't comment.

She was surprised to see the size of the crowds waiting to greet their ship, despite the late hour and the driving rain. First-Class passengers were escorted off the ship first, the photographers' flash lamps lighting up the otherwise dark night. She didn't envy the attention those poor women were getting. Everyone wanted to know about the rich men who had died. It seemed America was no different than Ireland in that respect, where those with money appeared to be more valuable.

Then she heard some of the questions the reporters were asking, their voices carrying on the wind.

"Is it true the officers shot people dead?

"Did passengers get into gunfights?"

Delia and Conor exchanged a look of disbelief. How could anyone ask questions of that sort? When it came to their turn to leave, they put their heads down and ignored the questions fired in their direction. A long line of ambulances were waiting, and Conor was taken to Saint Vincent's Hospital. Delia refused to be left behind. She went with him.

At the hospital, a nun took Conor away, telling Delia to sit in the waiting room. She paced back and forth before going looking for her husband.

She found Kate and Cathy. Cathy appeared to be asleep, with Kate sitting by Cathy's bedside. Kate fidgeted, passing her rosary beads from one hand to the other. She glanced at Cathy, before turning to Delia.

"Cathy spoke to me, at last." Tears made Kate's eyes glisten. "Her sister hasn't come to see her yet. Cathy is convinced she blames her for Seamus dying, but, sure, what woman would believe that?"

"Given how my aunt behaved, Kate, I am rarely surprised by what people believe."

Delia kicked herself as Kate's face lost what little color it had left. Delia hastened to reassure her. "It's early yet. The sheer numbers of people waiting for the ship must have caused delays. I'm sure Cathy's sister will be here as soon as she is able."

From what little Kate had told her about Cathy's sister, Delia hoped she was right. But she didn't have time to deal with it now.

"Kate, I will come back to see you in a while. Where are you staying?"

"Here. I've been sneezing. It's only a cold, but the doctor wants me checked out." Kate glanced around her before whispering. "I'm relieved. I didn't want to have to look for somewhere on my own."

"You could have stayed with me. The nun, on duty in the waiting room, suggested a hotel across the street." Delia spotted a nun walking out of a ward. "Sorry, Kate, that nun over there is looking after Conor."

Delia went to find her husband. He was settled in a ward along with other survivors. She kissed Conor before taking a chair beside his bed.

"Delia, this is Thomas Whitely and John Thompson, both crew members from the *Titanic*."

Thomas spoke first. "Evening, ma'am. Forgive me, if I don't get up to shake your hand. Be a while before I'll be walking anywhere."

Delia smiled at the weak joke. She assumed his leg was broken given it was elevated. His arms were wrapped in bandages. "What did you do on the ship, Mr. Whitely?"

"I was a waiter. Lucky to be here. Thanks in no part to my best mate here. Never knew his name before the sinking. Johnny's a fireman. He broke his arm, saving me."

John didn't appear to enjoy the praise. He seemed to tunnel under his bedcovers. The nun arrived back on the ward. She gave a pointed look at the clock. Delia took the hint.

"See you tomorrow, darling." She kissed Conor on the cheek for the sake of decorum.

"Where are you staying?"

"At the hotel across the street. One of the nuns suggested it. She said quite a few of the families had booked in."

"Delia, have you heard from my brothers?"

"No, darling, but things are rather chaotic. The hospital staff has been told to only admit close family. I think they are afraid of the reporters."

CHAPTER 57

*H*aving been transferred to the *Lapland*, Gerry followed the smell of food.

Davy waved at him. "Gerry, come sit with us. Have you found out anything more about your friend, Tommy? I can't find anyone who saw my brother."

"Someone spotted him helping passengers with their lifejackets around One. Nobody remembers seeing him after that."

"Have you written to his family, or are you going to wait to speak to them in person?

"I tried writing, but gave up." Gerry put some butter on his bread roll. "When do we ship out?

"Gerry, didn't you hear? We're not allowed go back to England. They want us to stay in America."

Stunned, Gerry couldn't believe his ears. He didn't have the money for a holiday.

"Davy, who wants us to?"

"The man, Senator William Smith, who is heading

the inquiry, says he wants to speak to all the crew to find out what really happened. If you ask me, they think there is going to be a whitewash. Nobody wants to admit they did anything wrong. Those First-Class nobs, they'll sue and win millions for what they lost."

Another man spoke up. "True, Davy. I was a steward in First Class. Some fella had a car on board. He used to ask his man servant to go and check on it. When you think about all those diamonds, gold, jewelry, and other stuff that went down in the old girl."

Sickened, Gerry turned on them.

"Who cares what things went down on the ship. Fifteen hundred people died. Don't they deserve justice? Don't their families warrant the truth?"

The room fell silent, as everyone stared at him. He stood up to go cool down. Davy put his hand out to stop him.

"Of course, they do. But how can we help them? You got to be careful what you say, Gerry. The officers said we have to tow the company's official policy. Those that don't will never get another job with White Star Line again."

Gerry didn't care about working for White Star Line ever again. He had questions that needed answers. Why hadn't they had a lifeboat drill? Why weren't there enough spaces for everyone? Why did the ones that were there leave the ship half empty? Why did the captain order full steam ahead, when he knew they were in the middle of an ice field? Why, why, why? All the unanswered questions, all the ifs and buts were driving him mad. Sometimes, he wished he could just forget the whole thing, go back home and marry Jean. But how could he face Jean and her mam knowing that Tommy had died, and he'd lived?

"They can threaten what they like. I'll tell the truth no matter what they ask me. They knew we needed more lifeboats, but someone decided it would make the deck look cluttered. Cluttered!" He swore under his breath, his appetite gone, and walked outside to get some air. As soon as he opened the door, he remembered the photographers and reporters. They were offering all sorts of incentives for someone to talk to them.

He turned on his heel and bumped into Davy.

"Sorry, Gerry. I didn't mean to upset you."

"It's me who should be sorry. I took your head off." Gerry took a deep breath.

"You're not going to speak to the reporters, are you, Gerry?"

He shook his head. "No, Davy. I can't say I wasn't tempted. It would be one way of getting payback for our mates who died."

Davy still looked worried. "So, what are you going to do?"

Gerry held Davy's gaze. "As God is my witness, I am going to tell that senator everything he wants to know. Maybe, he can stop something like the *Titanic* happening again."

Davy stared at Gerry. "The officers won't like that."

"Let them off. It's their necks on the block. I wouldn't want to be in their shoes, when the inquiry asks why they didn't fill the lifeboats properly. Apart from Lightholler, how did the others survive?"

"They seem to have manned the boats. I guess they were ordered off by the more senior officers. Did you hear Murdoch committed suicide?" Davy sighed. "He said he couldn't live with the guilt of making the mistake and sending us crashing into the iceberg."

"Davy don't spread rumors like that. We don't know for sure. I didn't know the man well, but he didn't seem like the type to do that. It could have been Quarter Master, Hitchens, who made the mistake. He had control of the wheel. He didn't behave too well in the lifeboat, from what has been said. He told a lady to shut up, when she asked to go back to save some of those drowning," Gerry swallowed. He still couldn't believe anybody, but fifth-officer, Lowe, even tried to help those in the water. "When all is said and done, Murdoch died, and we should respect his memory."

Davy looked as if he would cry. Gerry hoped he wouldn't. He didn't know what to do if the man broke down.

He patted Davy on the back. "I understand how you feel. I feel the same way about Tommy. Why did he die, and I survived? Sit down, and I'll get us a cuppa tea."

Gerry didn't know if he believed what he was telling Davy or not. The events of the last few days and nights had turned his thinking upside down. He had placed huge faith in Captain Smith, having sailed under him many times. Yet it seemed he had known about the icebergs and yet ordered the engine rooms to increase to full speed, anyway. He brought the tea back to the table.

"I can't stop thinking about that night. The questions in my head, they are driving me mad."

Davy stirred his tea but didn't look up. Gerry continued.

"We thought the ship was unsinkable, but did that give Captain Smith enough reason to take risks? Was that why he canceled the lifeboat drill?"

"Would having a drill have made a difference?"

"Who knows? Maybe the lifeboats would have been full leaving the ship? Lightholler wouldn't let men on the boats, even if there were no women left. Murdoch let everyone on. Yet they were supposed to follow the same rules?"

Davy interrupted him. "Gerry, you need to get some sleep. Can't be thinking like that. It will drive you mad."

"That's why I have to stay here, at least until the inquiry is over. I can't sleep. I just go over everything again and again. Maybe someone more intelligent than me will be able to give me answers."

CHAPTER 58

*S*t. *Vincent's Hospital, New York*

Kate and Cathy had both been admitted to St. Vincent's hospital. The doctors examined them both for signs of frostbite. Feeling better after a good night's sleep, Kate took a chair beside Cathy's bed. A nun was taking Cathy's temperature.

"Sister, what did the doctor say about Cathy?"

The nun pushed the hair back from Cathy's face.

"Poor girl. He says she is in shock."

Kate gripped the side of her chair. "The other nun said a survivor went mad from shock. That woman was sent somewhere else."

"Don't court trouble, dear. Your friend is young and seems healthy enough. Like most of the survivors, she should recover in time. My guess is she doesn't want to face her loss."

"She was very close to her brother."

The nun wrote something down. "I have to go, but keep talking to her. Some doctors believe people who appear to be unconscious can still hear us."

SOMETIME LATER A DIFFERENT nun came into the ward. "Kate, there's a man by the name of John Donnelly, asking for you. Come with me, please."

Kate hung back. He could only be Daniel's brother. What would she say to him?"

The nun looked behind her to find Kate not following. "Come along, girl, I have things to be doing."

Kate followed the nun more out of obedience than anything else. The reception area was crowded. How would she find John Donnelly? She looked around, and then her heart stilled, as a man the spitting image of Daniel walked toward her. He held out his arms, and she found herself hugged tight.

"'Tis a sight for sore eyes, you are, Kate Maloney. I'd barely recognize you, except for those green eyes of yours. Let me look at you. You aren't hurt are ye? The nurse said one of the girls was very ill."

"She meant Cathy Madden. She isn't coping very well with the loss of her brother and..." Kate stopped speaking. She couldn't talk about Daniel, not to his brother.

"Danny wrote to me about you. He said he hoped to talk you into moving west with him. Did he mention it to you on the ship?"

Kate nodded.

"Will you come out and grab a bit of lunch with me? You look half-starved." He cleared his throat, his cheeks flushed. "I don't want to make things difficult for you, but I'd love to know what happened to my brother."

"I will, but can you wait a few minutes. I need to tell Cathy where I am."

"I'll wait here, until you come back. Take as long as you need."

Kate walked away, without glancing behind her. She knew he was looking at her, and she could feel his gaze on the back of her neck. It was weirdly comforting he was so like Daniel. She didn't feel so alone now.

She picked up the Arran sweater she had left by Cathy's bed. Why hadn't Bridie come to see her sister? Not that Cathy would notice. Kate couldn't help wondering, if seeing her sister would bring Cathy back to her old self.

Kissing her friend on the cheek, she whispered she would be back in a while. There was no response. Cathy just lay there with her eyes closed.

When she returned to reception, John, or Sean as she remembered him, was waiting just as he said he would.

"Let me take your arm. There are crowds of people around including some reporters who seem to care about nothing but getting their story."

"Don't tell them I am a survivor. I keep telling them I am just visiting, and they'll leave me alone then."

"You aren't just a pretty face, are you?" He glanced at her, admiration lighting up his eyes. She blushed at his flattery. Then she felt the Arran sweater.

"This was Daniel's. He gave it to me to keep me warm. He insisted I take it. Maybe, he should have kept hold of it."

"It is not your fault, Kate Maloney. My brother died because of the White Star Line, plain and simple. You couldn't have saved him any more than you could have saved the rest of those lost souls. I am only glad Cathy and you were able to save yourselves."

Sean, she couldn't think of him as John, walked on the outside of the pavement or sidewalk, as he called it. The silence between them wasn't uncomfortable. Feeling overwhelmed by the noise and the crowds of people dashing up and down the streets, Kate was glad he didn't try to make conversation.

They sat down at a restaurant. He handed her the menu.

"Pick what you like, my treat."

Kate wasn't hungry.

"Kate, you have to eat. You'll fall ill, otherwise."

"I'll have pancakes." She wasn't quite sure what they were, but she couldn't face anything else.

While waiting for their food, Sean kept her amused, by telling her different stories about his time in New York.

It didn't take long for their meal to arrive. She looked up, trying to squeeze back the tears in her eyes.

He took her hand. "What's wrong?"

"They're like Nell's griddle cakes. I miss her." How she wished the old woman was with her now. She needed her guidance and strength.

"I'm sure you are finding things difficult, what with Cathy being in the hospital and you a stranger in America. I can't stay for long, but I can stay for a couple of days, if it helps."

She looked up at him. "Sean, I'm grateful for your offer, but you don't have to stay away from your family. I have to learn to stand on my own two feet."

"Kate Maloney, will you stop. We are family – all of us from Ballinasloe. You just have to be from Ireland to be part of the Irish family in America."

When she didn't laugh at his joke, he stopped smiling. He ran a hand through his hair. "Sorry. I make jokes when I get nervous. Why don't you tell me what happened? It may help to talk about it. But don't feel you have to."

Kate found herself telling Sean everything about the *Titanic,* even bits she hadn't realized she remembered until now. He was a good listener, staying quiet even when she became upset. He simply held her hand and gave her his hanky. Letting her cry made it easier than having to bottle everything up. When she told him about Daniel putting her in the lifeboat, he coughed. She thought she saw a tear escape, but that was it.

After she finished, they sat in comfortable silence for a while before Sean asked her, "What will you do now, Kate?"

Kate played with her cup. She didn't know what to say. She had no idea, and the thought terrified her.

"Please talk to me. Maybe I can help in some way. I

certainly can't leave New York without making sure you will be all right. I owe Daniel that much." Sean smiled.

He was being very kind, but Daniel hadn't promised her anything.

"Anyway, Nell would come over on the next ship and kick my backside, if I left her precious girl alone."

Kate laughed for the first time in what seemed like forever. He was right. Nell would have a fit, if any of their neighbors didn't look out for her. But what did he mean, when he left New York?

She vaguely remembered Daniel telling her Sean lived on a farm. "You don't live in New York?"

"No, I don't. I hate this place. I live in Riverside Springs, Wyoming. When I heard the news of the sinking, I came in the hope that Daniel was among the survivors. When I found out he wasn't..." Sean looked away for a couple of seconds. Then he continued talking, "I went back to my hotel, where I met a lady called Delia Brennan. She told me about Cathy and you and how Daniel helped ye. I couldn't leave New York without checking Cathy and you were all right. I am not leaving until you tell me your plans."

"I don't have any." Kate put her hand up to her mouth, not quite believing she had just told him the truth. But once she started speaking, she couldn't stop. "I was meant to live with Cathy, but her sister doesn't want me. I found out from a letter on the *Titanic*. That's when Daniel, well, he asked me to marry him and go live near you. I forget where he said, but he wanted to work with horses. Now Cathy is here, and she is really ill. Her sister hasn't even come to see her, and I don't know what to do."

Sean didn't look at her, but his grip on his cup tightened, and she could see the whites of his knuckles.

"Bridie Madden was always a cold fish. She wouldn't give you the time of day, unless there was something in it for her. Don't mind her. You wouldn't want to be beholden to that one. What is the story about Cathy? Was she injured?"

Kate shook her head. "The doctor says it's a combination of shock and a broken heart. She was very close to Seamus, you know."

Sean nodded. "Aye, she was always following him around when we were youngsters." He fell silent for a couple of seconds before adding, "Why don't you both come with me? I live near a lovely town called Riverside Springs in Wyoming. It's small but growing and has a great sense of community. It's a bit like at home. Everyone knows everyone else, a bit too much sometimes." He smiled to let her know he was joking.

She didn't respond, not quite believing he was offering her a chance at a new life. She didn't have to do this alone.

"I have a farm with horses. It's not big, but there is plenty of work in the town for us. Declan is married to a lovely woman called Mary. She'd love some female company on the farm. She doesn't have a lot of time to go visiting with the other ladies in town. Mary would also be a chaperone, so Nell would be happy. You wouldn't be living with two bachelors in the middle of nowhere."

Kate was about to say Nell would be happy to know she was with someone she knew from back home, but Sean hadn't finished.

"There is work to be had in Riverside Springs. Mrs. Grayson runs a store and a hotel. To be honest, she is getting on a bit, but she is a stubborn old woman and refuses to admit she needs help. She'll remind you of Nell. You could work there, if you fancied that idea." He pressed his lips together, staring intently into her eyes. "You can't stay here in New York. Not with no one looking out for ye. You could be sold to the white slavers or worse."

Kate stared at him. White slavers? He had to be joking. It couldn't be that bad, surely?

"Kate, this city isn't for those as innocent as you and young Cathy, not without a man looking out for you. Now, why don't we go back to the hospital and speak to the doctor? Maybe he would agree that some country air and good living would do Cathy a world of good."

Kate felt everything was rushing past her so fast. She loved the picture he painted of his town, but to move out of New York when it was all Cathy had wanted. Cathy wasn't the same as the girl who left Ballinasloe. And what about her own life? She didn't like New York. Granted she had only seen a small bit of it, but it was too busy for her. She preferred a quieter area just like home. She wanted to be in Galway, but there was no way you would get her on a ship again.

Sean looked at her expectantly. She wasn't quite ready to say yes. She wanted to, but...

"What about Bridie?" she heard herself say, despite her hopes rising. Sean Donnelly could help her with Cathy, and maybe her friend would recover.

"What about her? Cathy can write to her parents once she settles. I will drop a line to Nell and the Maddens to reassure them I have taken you under my wing. Although come to think of it, that might be enough to get Mr. Madden over here and take ye home. He mightn't like his daughter mixing with the Donnellys."

Kate smiled at the reference to his history. With his brothers in prison for fighting the English and the rest in America, some of the locals back home thought the Donnellys were trouble. Nell thought they were heroes and didn't make any bones about it. She didn't know what Mr. Madden's views were. It had never come up in conversation.

"Nell was always very fond of your family. She often said you and your brothers reminded her of her boys."

"She's a wise lady, although I didn't get involved in the fighting. I can't stand violence for any reason."

"What?"

"I'm sorry. I forgot your dad died with Nell's sons fighting the English."

"My father made his choices. They wouldn't be mine. I don't like Ireland being under the control of England, but I don't believe in killing anyone either."

His smile lit up his whole face, making his eyes shine even more. Her stomach did a summersault, which unnerved her more than the expression in his eyes.

"So, are you game? Will you come home with me?"

"Home with you?" Sometimes you had to take a chance, and something told her this was the right choice to make. "Yes, I will come with you to Riverside Springs."

SEAN PAID the bill and escorted Kate out of the restaurant. He stopped walking and put his finger under her chin, so she looked at him.

"I'm so glad you are coming home with me and not just because it would make Daniel happy, if he's looking down on us. I couldn't leave you here in New York. I wouldn't be able to sleep at night."

Kate stilled. He sensed her withdrawal and drew away from her.

"What did I say?"

"Sean, you do not have to look after me. I'm a grown woman, and I've got a mind of my own. I appreciate your care and concern, and I will go to live in Riverside Springs, but I will fend for myself."

"Yes, ma'am." He mock saluted her in the street, causing passers-by to look at him. She giggled at his antics and for a brief few seconds forgot the tragedy that had brought them here to this street.

The guilt descended just as quickly. What right did she have to be laughing, when Cathy was in the hospital and Daniel and Seamus at the bottom of the ocean?

"Kate, don't do that."

"Do what?" she said, afraid her facial expressions were so easy to read.

"Feel guilty. You survived for a reason. Daniel and

Seamus didn't. I don't know why it happened, and I will miss my brother for the rest of my life. But he would want us to go on living. Now, let's go find Cathy. The girl I remember was full of life. If anyone can help her return to her full health, it's you."

CHAPTER 59

*W*hen they returned to the hospital, they were surprised to find Bridie visiting Cathy. Kate and Sean exchanged a glance. Sean held out his hand.

"Bridie, it's been a long time. I'm sorry about Seamus."

Bridie shook his hand but didn't mention Daniel. She leaned in, as if to kiss Kate on the cheek, but missed. Kate didn't know what to say. Had Bridie come to offer her a place to stay? Or a job? Was she going to take Cathy home with her?

"Sean, have you completed the forms yet?"

Kate glanced at Sean. What forms? Sean looked just as puzzled as she was.

"Forms?"

"Don't be coy, Sean Donnelly. We all know what your family is like."

Sean clenched his jaw, his eyes narrowing.

"What do you mean by that?"

Bridie turned back to pick up her coat from the chair by Cathy's bed. For once, Kate was glad her friend appeared oblivious to what was going on around her. Bridie was in a funny mood.

"It's all over the papers. Awards are being made to the victims of the *Titanic*, the survivors as well as those who died."

Sean spoke through gritted teeth. "Mother Mary of God, Bridie Madden. Our brothers are barely dead a week. How could you think of money at a time like this?"

Bridie dismissed his comment with a look. Kate took a step between them.

"Bridie, are you taking Cathy home to live with you?" Kate asked.

Bridie's color faded to match the linen on the bed. "No, the doctors don't believe that would be in Cathy's best interests. They are moving her to Bellevue."

Sean's intake of breath surprised Kate.

"What is Bellevue?" Kate's heart beat faster, as Sean glared at Bridie.

"Seems Bridie is putting her sister in a mental asylum." Sean spat out the words.

Kate recoiled. She couldn't believe what she was hearing. Nobody put their family in one of those places, not unless they really were insane. Cathy just needed some fresh air, plenty of good food, and some time to recover from the shock of losing everything, including her brother.

"You can't. Why would you do that? Cathy just

needs some care and love to help her recover. She doesn't need to be locked up." Kate pleaded, not caring she sounded desperate. She'd read about lunatic asylums in Ireland, and she didn't want anyone she knew to live in one, least of all someone as full of life as Cathy had been.

Bridie stood up, patting down her black skirt and flicking something from her white blouse. Kate examined her but couldn't see any resemblance to the girl who had left Galway all those years ago. She had similar coloring to Cathy, but that was all. Cathy looked like she belonged on stage, with her mesmerizing smile and dancing eyes. Bridie's eyes were the same color but lacked any depth or emotion. She stared back at Kate, as if they were discussing the weather, not the future of her sister.

"You can't. Please don't do this." Kate knew she was begging, but she didn't care.

Bridie turned away. Over her shoulder, she said, "I don't have time to look after her. I have a job and a life of my own, you know."

Kate couldn't think straight. She had to do something to stop this from happening, but what?

"I'll take her. Kate is coming to Riverside Springs with me. Cathy will love it there. Plenty of everything she needs to recover."

Bridie turned on Sean, and her face screwed up in temper. "So that's your game, is it, Donnelly? Not content to claim for the loss of one brother, you aim to deprive me of my dues. I won't stand for it, do you hear me?"

Kate watched, as the color left Sean's face briefly, before he clenched his hands into fists. He didn't raise his voice, which made his words even more chilling.

"Bridie Madden, if you were a man, I would take you outside and punch you for what you are doing. You always were a mean-spirited young one, and it seems maturity has only made you worse. Kate, I will wait for you outside. I can't share the same air as that one."

"Good riddance, Donnelly," Bridie spat after him. Kate rushed to Cathy's side and, taking her hand, tried to get her friend to listen.

"Wake up, Cathy. Daniel's brother is going to take care of us, both of us. He will take us to his farm. It's out in the countryside, and we will have time to heal. Open your eyes, please." Despite Kate's begging, Cathy lay lost in her trance.

Bridie sniffed. "See, there's nothing anyone can do for her. At least in Bellevue they are trained to deal with people like her." She paused before asking Kate, "Do you know what she had in her luggage?"

Kate just stared at her, her mouth open but no words would come. Bridie took up a pen and a piece of paper. She completely ignored Kate. Kate glanced at Cathy. She had to fight for her friend.

"Jesus Mary and Joseph, she's your sister, for goodness sake. She came all the way over here to be with you. You can't send her to that place."

Bridie's tone could have given Kate worse frostbite than the ocean water.

"It is of no concern of yours what I do, Kate

Maloney. Now please leave. Your presence is upsetting my sister." Bridie turned to the nearest nurse. "This woman is no longer allowed to visit my sister. I will be back tomorrow."

The nurse looked at Kate with pity in her eyes, but she couldn't go against the family. Kate picked up her bag and Daniel's sweater. She kissed Cathy's forehead goodbye. She signed herself out of the hospital and went to find Sean.

When he saw her coming, he held his arms out for her, and she went to him willingly. She cried tears of frustration, anger, and loss, before she could compose herself.

"We will write to the Maddens and tell them the truth of what has happened. Come on now, let's get back to my hotel. We will get you a room for tonight and head home tomorrow."

She nodded, glad someone else was making the decisions for her. She couldn't think straight. Her head hurt, as much as the pain in her chest.

CHAPTER 60

*W*hen they returned to Sean's hotel, she was pleased to bump into Delia Brennan.

"I am so glad to see you Kate. Conor is being released from the hospital tomorrow." Delia kissed her friend's cheek.

"This is Sean, Daniel's brother."

"Nice to meet you, Sean." Delia shook Sean's hand. "I am very sorry for your loss."

Sean nodded. Delia turned back to Kate. "Have you made plans yet, Kate?"

"She is going to come home with me. I have a farm in Wyoming – my brother and me. Kate has known us since she was a baby. Mary, my sister-in-law, will look after her, fatten her up, and let her rest."

"And Cathy?" Delia asked, her eyes wide with curiosity. Kate let a sob escape. She couldn't bear to talk about what had happened. Delia took her by the arm and led her to a seat. Sean muttered something about getting some tea and left.

"I'm sorry, Delia. Cathy is being sent to Bellevue. It's a hospital for those who have lost their minds. Only, she hasn't. I don't think she needs anything more than patience and some loving care. But her sister, she won't listen to Sean or me. She told us to leave."

"I am so sorry. I know how close you girls were. Maybe you can go back tomorrow to see her."

"No. Bridie told the staff we weren't to be let in. The nurse said they had to obey Bridie. I can't do anything. I feel like I failed Cathy."

Delia bristled. She knew just how horrid families could be. She only had to look at her Aunt Cecilia. The poor girl in front of her had already been through so much. She didn't need this extra burden of guilt.

"You didn't, Kate. You have been through an ordeal yourself, and alone you can't fight this. If you don't want to go with Sean, you are very welcome to stay with us. I only just met Conor's family, but they seem nice. They are going to help us find a home and jobs. They would help you, too. I'm sure of it."

Kate rubbed the tears away with Delia's hanky. She noticed her friend was wearing a new dress, not the one donated to her by the people on the *Carpathia*.

"Thank you, Delia, but Conor and you are just starting your lives together. I will be fine with Sean. I've known his family all my life. I don't have a lot of memories of Sean, as he left home years ago, but, from what I remember, he is a very good man. Declan, Daniel's older brother, has a good reputation back home, too. I know they will look out for me."

Delia grasped her hand.

"Make sure to give me his address. I'd like to write to you, if you don't mind. I would hate to lose contact. I know we only met on the ship, but it feels like we have been friends for years."

"It seems like a lifetime, since we left Queenstown."

"Did you hear they are holding an inquiry?"

"I didn't know that. I don't think I can talk about anything without crying. I just want to forget about that night. Those screams. The whole thing," Kate put her face in her hands and wept again.

Delia pulled her into a hug, and that's how Sean found them.

"I got some tea, but maybe you need something stronger?" he asked. He pulled at his collar, after he put the tray on the table in front of them.

"No, thank you. Tea is lovely, Mr. Donnelly. Could I take your address, so I can write to Kate? I believe you are leaving first thing in the morning."

Kate saw the look of relief on Sean's face.

"Yes, ma'am. I think it's best to get away from the reporters and everything and give Kate a chance to recover."

Delia nodded. "I understand. I swear if another reporter shoves his camera in my face, he may just end up eating it."

Kate giggled. She couldn't imagine someone as lady-like as Delia getting violent. She'd had long conversations with Cathy about Delia and how she looked like she belonged in First Class. Cathy had mimicked how Delia walked and talked. It had all made sense when Delia explained about her aunt and how she had eloped.

"Did you make contact with your family back home?" Kate asked.

Delia cringed. She felt guilty for not letting her aunt know she was safe, but she didn't want to risk her upsetting her new life.

"I sent a telegram to Geraldine. It's up to her whether she tells my aunt, but, given she didn't know I was on the *Titanic*, I see no point really."

"But what if the papers print a list of survivors?"

Delia shrugged her shoulders. "They have but only those in First Class. It seems America isn't that different to Ireland, after all."

Sean looked up at her remark. "Senator Smith is trying to change that, Mrs. Brennan. He intends to hold the White Star Line responsible for the fact that more steerage passengers died than in any other class. The crew had a better survival rate than men like my brother."

Delia nodded. "Indeed, it would appear so. But I do hope the inquiry also acknowledges the actions of the brave crew members who did so much to get us to safety. People like Mr. Hart, the steward who escorted me to the boat deck. He returned below to bring up the second group of people, even when it looked like all was lost. The officers and crew members who filled the boats must have been tempted to save themselves but didn't. Even

Mr. Ismay, who the press has convicted without a trial, helped get women and children off that ship."

Kate shuddered, as she struggled to stop herself going over the events of that night. Yet she owed the men and women who had worked so hard to save them.

"I met a member of the black gang, as they call them on the *Carpathia*. He lost his brother, an engineer, on the ship."

"We can't forget the band. None of them survived." Delia pointed to a picture of the men standing with their instruments. "The reporter says some priest who got off in Queenstown took this picture. I hope their families got copies."

"They keep talking about the band playing *Nearer My God to Thee*. I didn't hear that from my boat. I heard the music but didn't recognize the tune. Did you?" Delia looked at Kate.

Kate shook her head. She knew they had played music, but she didn't know what it was. She'd had enough talking about that night.

"Thank you, Delia, for everything." Kate finished her tea. "I think I need an early night." She glanced at Sean. He stood up.

"Yes, we have to take you shopping in the morning before our train leaves. You can't go to Wyoming without some basics. The local store doesn't stock a lot of women's necessities, if you get my meaning." Sean looked at the space above Kate's head, obviously uneasy.

Delia and Kate exchanged a private smile, as Sean turned bright red.

Delia leaned in to kiss Kate on the cheek. "I think you will be in very safe hands, Kate. Be happy."

"You, too. Tell Conor I said goodbye."

Kate made arrangements to meet Sean for breakfast and then left for the room Sean had booked for her. It was so pretty with its blue and white colors, but she didn't appreciate any of it. She cried her eyes out for the loss of her friend. She couldn't help wondering, if it would have hurt more if Cathy had died on the ship. Her childhood friend deserved so much more than to end her days in this nightmare.

CHAPTER 61

*G*erry wanted to be back in England with Jean, not stuck here at the inquiry. He waited with Davy and some of the other surviving crew members, to tell their story.

Davy looked up from his newspaper.

"Gerry, it says in the paper, Senator Smith is determined to blame every member of the crew for the sinking. It shows he's never worked as a crew member on a ship before."

"Why?"

"As if we were going to question an officer's order. If the officer said jump, that's what we did. You know it, I know it, and he needs to learn that fact fast. He's grilled Harold Bride, the poor wireless operator for ages. That man should be in the hospital with his injuries."

"Davy, you can't afford to lose your temper, none of us can."

Davy's eyes were like flint. "Did you see the state of

Bride's shoes? Yet the officers were all done up like a, like a..."

"Officer?"

Davy glared at him but, before he could say anything, another seaman piped up. .

"He's not crew, though, is he? He didn't have to answer to the officers. Some say he ignored a message from the *Californian* about the ice. He was too busy to listen to it."

"That wasn't him. It was Phillips, the one who drowned. They were paid a pittance for manning that wireless set. Maybe, they earned tips when they sent all those messages about stupid things, like who had dinner with whom on the *Titanic,*" Davy muttered.

Gerry attempted to smooth things over. "Perhaps things will change, and all wireless operators will be paid properly. I heard a rumor the senator wants twenty-four-hour coverage on the ships. If they had that, the *Californian* would have heard the SOS and come to our aid."

Davy glared at Gerry. Gerry didn't know what he had said wrong.

"What? I'm not the one making the decisions. I just think that's what he is likely to want."

"Can't be so sure of that. The *Californian* saw the flares, didn't they, and they didn't come. Why would hearing it on the wireless have made a difference to that Captain Lord?"

Gerry held his hands up. "Maybe, none."

"Now, if it was Captain Rostron, he would have done exactly that. I don't think anyone would have died or at least not as many, if the *Carpathia* had been as near as the *Californian*. Captain Rostron is a hero. He came to our aid, as fast as he could despite the risk."

Gerry nodded. "Some woman on the *Carpathia* made a collection for him. She says he will get a gold cup or something. The crew will get medals."

Gerry wondered if the inquiry would give out any medals to the crew from the *Titanic*. Somehow, he doubted that would happen. Davy lit up another cigarette.

"Can't believe there are those who still believe the *Californian* wasn't the ship near us. Fourth-Officer Boxhall saw the ship through his binoculars. That's why he called them using the Morse lamp and then discharged rockets. He had no reason to lie. Captain Smith, God bless him, told the lifeboats to head for the ship."

A seaman from the *Titanic* raised his voice. "Davy, they aren't going to admit that they stood by and let fifteen hundred people die, are they? Officers all stick together, and they tell the same lies."

Gerry couldn't agree more, but it was pointless saying anything. He picked up Davy's newspaper.

"Says here, the *Olympic* black gang refused to leave Southampton. The ship's passengers were all on board, but the lads refused to move. They are demanding lifeboats for everyone."

Davy took a long puff. "I thought they had started that anyway. Didn't someone say the Americans were doing it?"

Gerry shifted to avoid the smoke wafting toward him. "They did, but that was for ships leaving their ports. The *Olympic* is in *England*. It seems it was loaded with some old boats from the army and other places."

"The army? What would they need boats for?"

Gerry ignored the question, as he read more of the article. "I knew it. It says here Jackson is involved. He's reported as having put his hand through the canvas of one boat. No wonder the men won't sail."

"I'd have thought Jackson would have taken the risk, given he missed the *Titanic*. His missus must be fit to kill him."

Gerry smiled at the thought of Mrs. Jackson. For all her temper, she loved her husband, warts and all, and was probably thanking God he'd stayed in the pub and missed going on *Titanic's* first, and only, trip. He read on.

"They thought the rest of the crew would join them, but the officers ordered the gangplanks to be removed, so the rest of the crew couldn't leave the ship. They are going to charge the lads with mutiny according to this."

Davy crossed himself. "Mutiny? That's serious. You can do prison time for that. They don't hang you anymore, or do they?"

Gerry didn't know, but he didn't think it likely anyone would hang a sailor for refusing to get on a ship that wasn't carrying enough lifeboats. Not after the *Titanic*.

Davy ground his cigarette into the floor. "Bloody officers! Never think of anyone but themselves, do they? When do you think they will call us?"

"I don't know, Davy. They might just take a statement. You might not get a chance to speak in front of all those important people."

"I wouldn't mind speaking in front of those ladies. They liked Officer Lowe, didn't they? They kept giggling when he was talking. They think he's a hero."

"Well, he did go back for them in the water. There isn't any other officer you can say that about. At least he tried, even if he did leave it a bit late."

"True that."

CHAPTER 62

*G*erry was one of the last to be called. He took an oath on the Bible, glancing around the room, as he did so. The White Star Line representatives sat stone-faced to a man, all eyes on him. He pulled at the collar of the second-hand shirt he had been given to wear. Was it him, or was it really hot in the room?

"Mr. Walker, you were on duty in the boiler room?"

"Yes, sir."

Gerry couldn't help but notice how small the senator was in person. His voice was that of a much larger man. Smith looked tired but determined. Gerry sat straighter. He was going to do everything he could to help this man get justice for those who died, Tommy among them.

"Mr. Walker, have you sailed under Captain Smith before?"

"Yes, sir." Gerry relaxed a little. This wasn't too bad.

"Were you involved in boat drills on those sailings?"

"Yes, sir, like clockwork. They took place every trip."

"What about on the *Titanic?*"

Gerry sat up straighter. "No, sir."

"There were no drills, or you didn't take part in them?"

Gerry's mouth grew dry. "Both, sir. No drills took place during the voyage. I didn't take place in the one at Southampton."

"Why not?"

"They picked better seamen than me, those who could row a boat." At the senator's look of disbelief, Gerry tried to explain. "What I mean, sir, is that they pick the men best suited to manning lifeboats. They tested the boats in Southampton, but they weren't filled up with people and lowered into the sea."

The sweat running down the back of his neck was making him itch. He hoped the senator wouldn't have too many more questions. He wished he could change his shirt.

"You can't row a boat, yet you are a sailor?" Smith's question caused some of the female observers to laugh.

"I'm a fireman, sir. Most of us are not sailors. Few crew members would know how to row a boat. Don't get much use for it, usually, sir."

Gerry hadn't meant to be amusing, yet the audience laughed again at his response. He hoped the senator didn't take offense. He'd heard this small man with the loud voice rip others to shreds.

"I see. Surely you did lifeboat drills when you were at sea, on other ships?"

"Normally, we would perform drills, but not on the

Titanic. It was due to take place on Sunday morning, but it didn't happen." Gerry glanced at the floor, not wanting to look at anyone.

"Why not?"

Gerry was about to tell him the captain didn't consult the firemen about his plans, but he stopped. This man was trying to do something others weren't and that was find out the truth behind what happened. He owed him his respect as well as his help.

"I have no idea. Some say it was because Captain Smith liked to give the Sunday sermon, at the First- and Second-Class service. Others say we didn't need it, because the ship was unsinkable."

"Obviously, it wasn't," someone shouted. Smith roared for silence, leaving Gerry feeling even hotter.

"Please go on, Mr. Walker."

"May have helped, though, if people had known where to find their boats. But then maybe not, as they would have then realized there weren't enough lifeboats for everyone. That would have caused panic." For a split second, Gerry wished he could go back in time and not say what he just had.

The senator eyed him for a few moments, which seemed more like hours. The White Star Line representatives glared at him. He guessed they didn't like what he was saying, but he didn't care. It was the truth.

"In your opinion, was everything done that could have been done to save all the passengers?"

Gerry fisted his hands and shuffled in the seat. He was tempted to respond that a low-ranking crew member wouldn't know the answer. But this was his chance to give his opinion on what happened. Should he take the easy option, or should he tell the truth, as he saw it. He played for time. "What do you mean, sir?"

"You are an intelligent man. I am sure you have read the newspaper coverage of the events of the night of the fourteenth. You will also see that the crew members' chances of survival mirrored those of the First-Class women and children. Those facts could make people think the crew took more care tending to themselves than to the people who paid for tickets."

Gerry bristled, his nails biting into the palms of his hands. He struggled to keep his tone civil. "Not the lads I worked with, sir. They kept working down below in an effort to keep her, the ship, afloat until a rescue ship came along. They were ordered up on deck. They weren't to blame for the lack of passengers in the boats."

"Then who was?"

Gerry stared at him. He had walked himself into this one right enough. He looked toward the White Star Line representatives, who now looked ready to swing for him. He cleared his throat.

"I think it was a mixture of things, sir." Gerry stopped for a moment. Should he keep talking or just leave it at that? For a second, Tommy's face popped into his mind. He had to do something, if only for Jean's brother.

Before anyone could stop him, he started speaking more rapidly.

"I think there is a lot of blame to be laid at other

people's feet. There should have been more lifeboats on the ship. There should have been a drill. The lifeboats should have been full before they left the ship." Gerry stopped talking as silence reigned. He wiped his forehead with a hand, before the sweat poured into his eyes.

After what seemed like a lifetime, but was only a minute or two, Senator Smith addressed him once more.

"What else, Mr. Walker?"

"That's about it, sir. I know there are other things that need to change. I don't claim to be an expert, but I think changes need to be made."

Smith shuffled some papers in front of him. "Now tell me how you came to leave the ship."

Was Smith implying he had shirked his duty? Gerry counted to ten to control his temper. "I didn't have much choice, sir. I was ordered onto a boat. On the ship, you have to follow orders, just like in the army."

"An officer ordered you into a lifeboat?"

"Yes, sir. First Officer, Murdoch."

"Did you refuse?"

Gerry's mouth fell open. Was the man mad? Who would refuse an order, but even more relevant, who would give up the chance to be saved? He'd wanted to live. He wanted a chance to see Jean, and get married, and have a family. The tears crept into his eyes, and he couldn't speak. He rubbed a sleeve across his eyes.

"Do you need a break, Mr. Walker?"

"No, sir, sorry, sir." Gerry pulled himself together. If Jean could see him now, she would be ashamed of him, a grown man crying like a babe.

"I wanted to live, sir."

Muttering broke out in the courtroom. Senator Smith did nothing to stop it. Gerry stared straight ahead, not looking from left to right, not making eye contact with anyone.

Gerry stayed silent, taking some deep breaths. He tried to stop his knees from shaking by pressing his feet firmly to the ground. How long would it take for the senator to ask another question? Senator Smith looked up.

"Did the lifeboat you were in go back for any passengers once the ship went down?"

"No, sir." Gerry stared at his shoes.

"Did you not hear the people screaming?"

Gerry closed his eyes, hearing and seeing the sounds from that night. His shirt, drenched now, stuck to him. He had to breathe slowly, as his heart pounded.

"Yes, sir. I asked the senior crew member to go back, but he said the ladies wouldn't like it."

"The ladies?"

"Yes, sir. He didn't specify which ones. I suggested to the ladies sitting near me that the screams could be their men and loved ones in trouble. Some were in agreement, but many were too frightened of what would happen."

"Please explain what you mean by that last remark, Mr. Walker?"

"The crew member, he said we would be swamped and the people in the lifeboat would drown. I tried, I swear I tried, to argue that wouldn't be the case. For a few minutes in the cold water would be enough to rob them of their strength. We had room in our boat, not as much as in some, but we could, we should have returned."

Senator Smith stared at him, an expression of pity on his face. Gerry didn't want this man feeling sorry for him. He just wanted to go home, back to England and Jean.

"Thank you for your assistance, Mr. Walker. You are excused."

Relieved, Gerry walked down from the stand and out of the inquiry room. It was pointless waiting for the other crew members or their bosses. He had finished his own career by telling the truth in that room, but he didn't feel bad about it. If anything, he was relieved. He owed Tommy, and all his fellow crew members, and the passengers, to do anything he could to stop something like the *Titanic* disaster happening again. He had done his best. The rest was up to the senator and his inquiry. There would be an inquiry, too, back in England, but he doubted he would be called to give evidence, not after that performance.

CHAPTER 63

RIVERSIDE SPRINGS, WYOMING,
APRIL, 1913

K ate Maloney wiped her hands down her gown once more. She had never had anything so beautiful.

"If you keep doing that, you will leave sweat marks on the dress. All brides are nervous, but, sure, Sean Donnelly loves the very bones of ye."

Her matron of honor and soon to be sister-in-law fussed around her like a mother hen.

"I know, Mary, but it seems so sudden. It's only been a year since the *Titanic*." Kate's voice trailed off. She hated talking about the ship.

"Sure, it was obvious the two of you were meant to be together. From the very first day you arrived. He went to New York for a reason. He may not have known it at the time, but it was destiny for you two to meet. Now, don't you think you have left the poor man waiting long enough?"

Kate turned to the woman who had offered her

friendship and love from that first day she had arrived in Riverside Springs, disheveled and heartbroken after the sinking. Mary had made her eat and drink and sleep, until she was convinced Kate wasn't going to fade away on her. It was Mary who had convinced Kate to take on the job of teaching the children, while their teacher, Mrs. Flynn, had her baby. Imagine her, Katie Maloney from Ballinasloe, ending up as a teacher! She'd written to Nell to tell her, but she wasn't sure if her adopted grandmother had gotten the letter prior to her death.

She still had Nell's last letter, though. Nell had dictated the letter to Father Curry to write on her behalf. Kate smiled at the thoughts of the priest writing about love and feelings. Nell had consoled her over the loss of Daniel but congratulated her on deciding to let Sean Donnelly take care of her. Nell had confided Sean would make a much better match for Kate, being that bit older and more mature. Kate pictured Sean walking across the meadow on his hands to make the school children laugh and wondered just how mature her husband to be was.

Nell had also given vent to her feelings about Cathy. It seemed the news of Bridie's treatment of her sister had spread through the whole parish and farther afield. Bridie would not be welcome any time soon should she decide she wanted to go home. Nell had written to say a memorial was going to be set up for the Burke family, so that John, Margaret, Ruth, Niamh, and little Sean would always be remembered. Daniel and Seamus were also going to have their own marker.

Nell had been thrilled with the money Kate had sent

her and wrote to say she had bought a new, warm shawl. Kate had asked Father Curry to pay the rent on Nell's house for another three months, her intention being to keep the woman who'd raised her from the workhouse. At least Nell had died in her own home. Kate hadn't wanted a penny compensation from the White Star Line. It didn't feel right, but Sean had insisted she take what was owed to her.

"Send it to Nell, if you don't want it, but don't let those idiots have it," he'd said. "You said you didn't want Nell in the workhouse, so you can use the money to prevent that from happening. You don't have to spend it on yourself."

She knew the money paid out for Daniel had gone back to Ireland to Mrs. Donnelly. Poor comfort for a woman who had lost so much already.

"What are you thinking about, Kate?"

She turned her attention back to Mary, who looked a little concerned.

"I was thinking of Nell, my adoptive grandmother, and how much she would have loved to have seen me get married."

Mary was on her knees fixing the hem of Kate's gown. She spoke through the pins in her mouth. "She's the lady who wrote to Sean?"

"What?" Kate pulled Mary to her feet. "Nell wrote to Sean? When?"

"He didn't tell you?" Mary looked stricken. "I'm sure he meant to. He was ever so touched. Nell, well the priest writing on her behalf, told him she couldn't think of a better man as a husband for you. She said you were the child of her heart. I remember that phrase, as I thought it was beautiful."

Tears filled Kate's eyes. She sent a quick prayer to heaven for Nell, before turning to the woman who had become her closest friend.

"Thank you, Mary, for everything."

"Ah, sure, I did nothing you wouldn't do." Mary sniffed. "You're welcome. I am so glad you will soon be an official part of our family. I just wish your friend Cathy could be here to see you."

Kate nodded. She'd been thrilled when Mr. Madden had written to say Cathy was out of Bellevue and on the way back to Galway. Reading between the lines of the letter, Cathy wasn't back to her usual self, but the hope was with the love of her parents and family she would recover. They had put in a claim for Seamus's life, and the money paid had covered the cost of the passage.

Kate patted the rosary beads in her pocket. They were never far away. Sean had made a special box for the clay Nell had given her. Nobody was allowed to make fun of that clay.

"Are you ready?" Mary asked.

Kate almost said yes but then remembered something. "I will be right back." She gathered up her skirt and walked quickly out of the church toward the graveyard. Picking her way through the graves, she soon reached the tree at the edge of the graveyard. Her eyes misted over, as she stared down at the marker.

"Thank you, Daniel, for helping me. Because of you,

I have found a man who loves the bones of me." She kissed a flower from her bouquet and laid it on the ground in front of the simple cross Sean had fashioned in memory of his brother. To the left of Daniel's marker was another one. She laid another flower on this one dedicated to Margaret Rice and her five boys. "If God blesses us with children, I hope they are as good as your boys, Margaret."

Then with a last look behind her, she made her way back into the church to start her new life as Mrs. Sean Donnelly.

CHAPTER 64

*G*erry Walker sat with his arm around his wife Jean, as they watched their baby boy, Tommy, play on a mat in front of the fire.

"Are you missing the sea, Gerry?"

Gerry glanced at the newspaper and cursed himself for bringing it home. Jean didn't need to see it. "No, darling, not a bit. I am that grateful for my new job. It means I can see more of you and my boy, don't it?"

Any time the *Titanic* was mentioned, Jean got upset. He'd put it down to pregnancy and her being emotional, but it went deeper than that. Jean searched his face, as if wondering if he was telling the truth. He took her hand and kissed it in an attempt to convince her.

"That it does. I couldn't bear for you to go back to sea, Gerry. It would put the heart across me every time you set sail. I'll never forget those days when we thought Tommy and you, God rest him, were dead. It was a miracle you came back to me, and I swore I would never let you out of my sight again." Jean turned to look him straight in the face. "Promise me you won't ever get on a ship again."

Taking a deep breath, he put his hand tenderly on her face and kissed her gently. "Jeanie, you know I wouldn't leave you out of choice, but there may come a time when I will be told to go. If that happens, I will have to obey orders."

She snatched her hand away and got up from the floor to sit on the sofa.

"You're talking about the war again, aren't you. What is it with men? They can't wait to march off to war."

She may sound angry, but he knew she wasn't. Not really. She was terrified. She'd told him what it had been like, those first few days after news of the *Titanic* had broken. At first, the families had been told all survived, but then the bad news had filtered through. Then he was kept in America for the inquiry, and she'd admitted she'd got to the point where she didn't believe she would see him again.

He hadn't known she was pregnant, when he left to go on the *Titanic*. She'd told him later. She'd been scared stiff of what would happen to her, an unwed mother. He thanked his lucky stars he'd survived and returned home to make an honest woman of her, as she called it. Their baby may have come early, but at least he wouldn't carry a stigma of illegitimacy for the rest of his life.

He moved the baby back from the rug in front of the fire to his cot, which was safer before taking a seat beside his wife.

"Jeanie, I've no interest in going to war. I pray every night it won't come to that, darling. But we can't be blind either. But let's not talk about that just now. Let's enjoy our wee man and our lovely house. We've been incredibly lucky, Jean Walker."

"I just hope it stays that way."

Gerry cuddled his wife and hoped her dream came true, but something told him, life as they knew it was about to change all over again.

CHAPTER 65

ONE YEAR LATER, NEW YORK, APRIL 15TH, 1913

*D*elia Brennan picked up the newspaper Conor brought home.

"Don't read it, love, some more upsetting stories in there. It's the anniversary and all."

She ignored his warning, her eyes focused on the picture of two boys.

"Conor, look these are the boys I told you about. They were with me in the lifeboat. The ones I couldn't understand. Says here they were kidnapped by their father. That's why they were on the *Titanic*."

Conor looked up from his dinner.

"Where is their mam?"

"She was in France, but they have been reunited now. They got their happy ending, I suppose."

Conor came up behind her, put his hands around her waist to cradle her stomach.

"We got ours, too, didn't we, darling? You, me and this little man of ours."

"How do you know it's a boy?"

Conor looked bemused for a moment. "I don't. I just assumed. I don't mind, if we have a girl. As I was saying, little did we know, when we arrived with only the clothes on our backs, things would turn out so well for us."

"I think that must be the understatement of the year. You got out of the hospital in no time at all. We didn't even have to wait long for the one hundred and twenty-five dollars from the American Red Cross. Some survivors are still waiting on claims to be paid out."

"Some of them have requested huge sums of money. I read one guy asked for over $10,000. He was in Third Class just like us."

Delia knew about the case. She had read a few different reports on the outlandish claims made by some survivors. "It's not our place to judge, darling. He may not have had any friends or relations to help him. We were lucky to have your brothers. Without them, you mightn't have found your job as quickly."

"They always need brickies in New York, Delia. They didn't find you a job in the store, did they? You did all that by yourself."

"Yes, but..."

"But nothing. You work hard, and the commission you earn means we could afford this apartment."

Delia looked around their new home. "Thanks, love. Not many men would acknowledge their wife's contribution."

"Not many men have a wife like mine, with her fine accent and fancy clothes."

Delia giggled, as he tickled her. "Nobody would ever have guessed we would settle so quickly, would they?"

Delia shook her head. "I love New York. I can't imagine living anywhere else. I know it's busy and noisy, but there is always something to do. Which reminds me, are you taking me to the circus this weekend?"

"Of course. Even the brothers want to come. That alright with you? I know you got a bit fed up of them, when we were sharing their place."

"Fine with me." Delia got on much better with Conor's brothers now they had their own place. She didn't have to see their dirty socks on the floor or clean up after them.

"I got a letter from Kate and another from John Hart, today. Kate said some reporters were hanging around wanting to talk to her."

Conor's face darkened. "They better not turn up here. I never want to discuss it, no matter how much money they offer me."

"Me neither. I won't be a party to gossip about anyone. Nobody knows how they would react in the same situation. And how is talking about it going to change anything."

Conor kissed her. "Don't get all het up, love. It's not good for the baby."

She changed the subject. "I got a letter from Geraldine earlier today. She said my aunt isn't doing so well. The doctors have diagnosed her with heart trouble." Delia knew Conor wouldn't have any sympathy for her aunt. She didn't keep secrets from him, although he wasn't a fan of her being in contact with Dublin. He worried her aunt would find a hold over her and come between them, as if she would let that happen.

"You mean they found a heart? Well, that proves miracles do happen!"

Delia knew she shouldn't, but she couldn't help laughing. She didn't blame Conor for his views on her Aunt Cecilia.

"Are you going to write back to Lady Fitzgerald to tell her about our son?" Conor asked, kissing the top of her head.

Delia turned into her husband's embrace. "There you go again. Our son!"

He kissed the top of her head.

"I don't know what we are having, and I don't care. I love you, Delia Brennan, and I already adore the child we are going to have. He or she will grow up surrounded by love, that much I promise."

Delia gave herself up to her husband's kiss, secure in the knowledge he meant every word.

AUTHOR'S NOTE

While most of the characters in this book and the circumstances they found themselves in, prior to boarding the *Titanic* are fictional, their experiences on board are inspired by real-life events.

Daniel Buckley, a Third-Class passenger, was the only Irishman to give evidence at the actual American inquiry. Senator Smith interviewed ex-crew on board their new ships, including Fred Barrett on the Olympic.

Buckley was one of the group who forced their way through the locked gates and up to the lifeboats. He boarded a lifeboat along with several other men. When the men were ordered out, at gunpoint, he lay on the bottom of the lifeboat. He credited Mrs. Astor with saving his life. She apparently threw a shawl over him, thus preventing anyone realizing he was there. Buckley joined the United States Army in 1917. He was killed by a sniper on 15 October 1918, while trying to retrieve wounded men.

Conor's experiences in the water are partly based on the true story of Patrick O'Keeffe, a young man from Waterford City. He had been living in America but returned to Ireland for a holiday to see his father. Patrick dreamed the *Titanic* would sink and his dream was so believable he tried but failed to sell his ticket. He sent a postcard to his family prior to boarding the ship.

"I feel it very hard to leave. I am down-hearted. Cheer up. I think I'll be alright – Paddy."

Patrick was still on board when the ship sank. He plunged into the sea from the steerage deck and pulled himself up onto what he described as a raft but was more likely a capsized Collapsible B. He testified he pulled on an Englishman and a Guernsey Islander, and then with their assistance they pulled on others from the water. According to local papers, he is credited with saving about twenty men and one woman. His claims were backed up by Harold Bride, the wireless operator from the *Titanic,* who told the tribunal a passenger appeared to be in charge of the raft. When Bride was asked how many were in the water trying to get onto the raft, his reply was 'dozens'. Patrick arrived in New York, battered and bruised, but alive. Locals in Waterford credit the fact he was a strong swimmer, who liked to swim in the cold, Irish Sea on Christmas Day, and his strength from his job as a porter, for his survival.

The Rice family, who appeared in this story, were real-life victims of the *Titanic.* The five boys were aged from two to ten years. Margaret Rice's body was recovered and buried, but none of her children were ever seen again. In her personal effects were a gold locket with a picture and a lock of hair, presumably that of her husband, and her rosary beads. Various survivors mention hearing the children pray at mass on the Sunday and then seeing them on deck with their mother moments before the ship split in two.

The French and Italian members of the catering staff were locked in their quarters and thus were prevented from leaving the ship. They were not officially crew, as they didn't work for the White Star Line but were employees of the restaurant. The members of the restaurant staff who did survive did so, because everyone assumed, they were passengers.

There is some controversy over whether the White Star officers shot and killed anyone on board. No bodies were recovered from the water with gunshot wounds. Irish survivors speak of shots being fired and men killed, they insist they were held back until the last possible moment, and more would have survived, if the women and children rule had been applied to Third Class. Letters from a First-Class passenger, George Reims, were found which also suggest that officers shot people. There were also hints at least one of the officers committed suicide.

The order to lower lifeboats came at 12:15 am, barely twenty five minutes after the strike. This was done more to comply with Board of Trade rules than a belief it would sink. However, the stokers and firemen from the front boiler rooms were among the first to be sent up top.

The passengers were huddled together in groups

praying. The priests led the prayers, causing some third-class passengers who survived to complain. They said the priests kept calling God to forgive the sinners, when these same sinners should have tried harder to save themselves.

The scenes depicted in the lifeboats combine elements from what occurred in different lifeboats on the Titanic.

Captain Ronston is on record talking about thanking God for taking him safely through the ice - when he stopped to take on the lifeboats' survivors, he counted circa 20 icebergs over 150 ft. tall and lots of growlers – 10- to 12-ft high.

The *Carpathia* and *Californian* met at 8:30 on Monday morning, just as the last of the Titanic lifeboats were being brought aboard. The ships communicated by semaphore. Captain Rostron thought one lifeboat was unaccounted for. Captain Lord said he would search around for it. Unfortunately, no more survivors were found.

A short prayer service took place on the *Carpathia* to thank God for the survivors and to pray for the dead. While this was going on, Captain Rostron maneuvered his ship around the wreck site. After about half an hour, he asked the *Californian* to continue the search. Captain Rostron sailed for some 56 miles to get around the ice, before setting a course for New York.

1912 was a very different era from today, and, although it is hard to believe, many Third-Class passengers wouldn't have expected to be treated any differently than they were. Some would have expected the boats to be filled in the following order – women and children, then First-Class men, Second-Class men, and so on.

The survival rates testify to the fact that some sort of segregation was in force. All but one of the First-Class children survived. The young girl who didn't was kept on board with her mother and father.

The children in Second Class were similarly saved, yet almost two-thirds of the children in Third Class drowned.

GLOSSARY

HEART OF DISASTER: DICTIONARY LIST

1. Banshees - In Irish legend, a female spirit whose wailing warns of an impending death in a house.
2. Bulkheads - a dividing wall or barrier between compartments in a ship
3. Chafed - rubbed briskly
4. Codladh sámh - sleep well
5. Collapsibles - wooden bottomed boat lined with cork, with canvas sides.

6. Craic - fun
7. Crossed themselves - made the sign of the cross
8. Cuppa - 'cup of tea' or other beverage
9. Cut-glass accent - high-class accent
10. Dampers – a valve or plate that stops or regulates the flow of air inside a duct or air-handling equipment.
11. Eejit - In Irish, a stupid person or an idiot - usually meant fondly.
12. Galwegians - people from Galway, Ireland

13. Growlers - a small iceberg

14. Het up - angry and agitated

15. Impish - Inclined to do slightly naughty things for fun, mischievous.

16. Joy - Mountjoy notorious Irish prison, in Dublin

17. Kit - uniform

18. Mam - mother

19. Maman - mama or mother (French)

20. Mass - Roman Catholic Service

21. Meself - myself 22. Our Father - the Lord's Prayer

23. Pillar box - mail box 24. Poop deck – The aftermost and highest deck of a ship. 25. Pride of place - Something is treated as the most important thing in a group of things.

26. Public house - Also known as a pub, an establishment licensed to sell alcoholic drinks.

27. Swamped - taken under the water by the strong pull of the boat and the currents

28. Tis -It is

29. Toffs - A derogatory word for someone with an aristocratic background, especially someone who exudes an air of superiority.

30. Wake - A funeral tradition associated with Ireland. It occurs from the time of death until the body is handed over to the church. It was a crucial part of the grieving process.

31. Ya - you

32. Ye - you

Clover Springs East

Writing as Ellie Keaton

ACKNOWLEDGMENTS

This book wouldn't have been possible without the help of so many people. Thanks to Erin Dameron-Hill for my fantastic covers. Erin is a gifted artist who makes my characters come to life.

I have an amazing editor and also use a wonderful proofreader. But sometimes errors slip through. I am very grateful to the ladies from my readers group who volunteered to proofread my book. Special thanks go to Marlene, Cindy, Meisje , Judith, Janet, Tamara, Cindi, Nethanja and Denise who all spotted errors (mine) that had slipped through.

Please join my Facebook group for readers of Historical fiction. Come join us for games, prizes, exclusive content, and first looks at my latest releases. Rachel's readers group

Last, but by no means least, huge thanks and love to my husband and my three children.

Made in the USA
Las Vegas, NV
20 August 2021

28472359R00187